Emily and Patch

Jessie Williams

Special thanks to
Thea Bennett

First published in 2013 by Curious Fox,
an imprint of Capstone Global Library Limited,
7 Pilgrim Street, London, EC4V 6LB
Registered company number: 6695582

www.curious-fox.com

Text © Hothouse Fiction Ltd 2013

Series created by Hothouse Fiction
www.hothousefiction.com

The author's moral rights are hereby asserted.

Cover Illustration by Ksenia Topaz
Illustrations by Dewi@kja-artists

ISBN 978 1 78202 020 2

1 3 5 7 9 10 8 6 4 2

A CIP catalogue for this book is available from the British Library.

Typeset in Baskerville by Hothouse Fiction Ltd

Printed and bound CPI Group (UK) Ltd, Croydon, CR0 4YY

MIX
Paper from
responsible sources
FSC® C020471

Emily and Patch

CITY FARM

Books in the
City Farm series…

Emily and Patch
Zoe and Swift
Darren and Basher
Katie and the Ducklings
Laura and Silky
Sammi and Dusty

For Janice, Shane and Vesty.

Prologue

Emily's eyes scanned the school hall. Below the stage, a sea of faces stared back up at her. The hall was packed. Rows of parents sat and waited for the Easter assembly to begin, but there was still no sign of her dad. Where was he? He'd promised her he'd be there.

Emily tried to remember the poem she was meant to recite. Something about clouds and daffodils. She'd told her teacher Miss Trimble that she didn't want to read, but she hadn't listened.

'It will be good for you to take part, Emily,' she'd said. 'You've been at Parkside for three months now – you need to join in more.'

But Miss Trimble didn't understand how hard it was to join in when you spent the whole time feeling like the wrong piece in a jigsaw puzzle. All of the other

 7

girls at her new school had their own friends, and they fitted together perfectly. But whenever Emily tried to talk to them her mouth would clam shut and her mind would go blank. Just like now.

She tried again to remember the first line of the poem, but it was no good. Yesterday she had known it off by heart, but today she was so tired her head was all woolly inside, and the words kept getting jumbled up.

There was a shuffling sound as the children from the reception class made their way up on to the stage. They were all holding hands and wearing floppy yellow bonnets that were supposed to look like daffodils.

As the little kids lined up in front of the painted backdrop of green fields and frolicking lambs, Miss Trimble waved at Emily from the side of the hall. *Now!* she mouthed, smiling encouragingly.

Emily dug her fingernails into her palms and forced herself to stand up. She felt dizzy and sick.

'I wandered...' she began, and the words drifted out and hung like a long, thin speech bubble over the listening faces. 'I wandered lonely as a cloud...' Emily took a deep breath. She'd remembered the first line at least, maybe now she'd be able to remember the rest.

Suddenly there was a commotion at the back of

the hall. Emily's dad came bursting through the swing doors. He was wearing his work suit and looking flustered. There was another clatter as Emily's stepmum Denise followed behind him, pushing the buggy. Everyone turned to see who was causing the noise. Emily felt her face begin to burn. It was so embarrassing, but at least her dad had made it. He gave her a quick wave. Emily felt her nerves begin to ease a little.

'I wandered—' she began again.

A loud wail rose up from the back of the hall.

Emily would know that wail anywhere. It was the same wail that had kept her up half the night. It was her baby half-brother Leon.

'I-I...' Emily stuttered. Behind her, she could hear some of the Reception kids start to giggle. She felt tears burning in the corners of her eyes. It was all going wrong again. No matter how hard she tried, nothing seemed to go well in this new school.

Flurgle-burgle, she imagined her mum whispering to her. *Flurgle-burgle* was the secret code word they had used when either of them felt like crying. It was so silly it would always make them laugh. But not this time. This time it only made her want to cry even more. A fat tear began trickling down her face. Then another and another. She saw her dad staring at her, his face creased with concern. She had to get out of there before things got any worse.

Blinded by tears, she stumbled across the stage.

'Emily!' she heard Miss Trimble call out after her. 'Emily, come back!'

But Emily didn't stop. She ran out of the side door and across the playground. She wanted to keep on running until she somehow made her way back to her old life. Her happy life with her mum.

But how could she? That life was over now.

Chapter One

Asha Gupta loved arriving at City Farm. Even though it was a cold and windy start to the Easter holidays, her heart was jumping with excitement at being back there again. She slammed the car door shut and waved goodbye to her mum. Then she tucked her lunchbox under her arm and looked up at the sign above the tall gates.

CITY FARM it said, in big green letters, surrounded by a border of painted animals.

Sometimes, when Asha stood outside the wrought-iron gates, she found it hard to believe that on the other side there was a real, live *farm*. That, sandwiched in between the flats and houses and busy roads and railways lines, there were stables and paddocks and animals. If it hadn't been for the Harvest Hope project, she might never have found out that the farm existed, let alone been able to come and work on it.

Icy drops of rain started to fall from the sky and Asha pulled her woolly hat down further over her head. Her hair was starting to grow back now but she still felt the cold a lot more than before she'd got ill. Back then, her shiny black hair had hung down to her waist. Her new short hair felt strange. Her mum said it was as lovely and soft as a kitten's fur, but Asha wasn't sure. She still liked to wear hats or scarves to keep it hidden.

She lifted the latch on the little wooden door at the side of the gates, and stepped through. As the door clicked shut behind her, she gazed around the farmyard. As it was the holidays, there were already a few early visitors pottering around, peering over the stable doors and *oohing* and *aahing* at the animals inside.

As soon as Asha started to walk across the farmyard, the chickens squawked and came flapping towards her on their long thin legs.

'Don't pretend you haven't been fed,' she said with a smile. 'I know Kerry's given you your breakfast.'

The birds stared up at Asha with their heads on one side, as if to say, *No way! Look – we're starving!* Asha sighed. With their shiny black eyes and pretty feathers, the chickens were just too cute to resist. She opened her lunchbox and looked inside. As usual, her mum had crammed it full of home-made goodies. The doctors had said that Asha needed to eat lots to get her strength back after her recovery from leukaemia, but there was no way she would be able to eat it all. Asha took a couple of veggie samosas, broke them into pieces and scattered them on the ground. The chickens pecked greedily at the crumbs in a blur of brown, black and orange feathers.

Asha giggled and carried on walking across the yard. As she drew level with the stables, Stanley, the black and white pony who was one of the oldest residents of the farm, poked his head over his door and neighed a loud greeting.

'Morning, Stanley,' Asha called. She was about to go over and scratch him under the chin when the door to the huge barn flew open and Rory Trent, the farm manager, stuck his head out. As usual, his cheeks were as red and shiny as two apples and his curly white hair sprouted from his head like clumps of cotton wool.

'Morning, Asha!' Rory's voice boomed across the yard, causing several of the visitors to jump. 'Get your skates on, lass. Meeting's about to start.'

And with that he disappeared back into the barn.

 13

Many years ago, before the city had started spreading outwards, the farm had been in the middle of open countryside. Although most of the original buildings had been knocked down and concrete blocks of council flats now loomed in their place, the ancient barn, with its thick stone walls and wooden beams, had survived.

The barn's uneven roof reminded Asha of the hunched back of an elephant, and its diamond-paned windows peered across the farmyard like eyes. It was like a wise old creature that had always watched over City Farm, keeping everything safe and happy. It was the perfect place for the Harvest Hope project and the children who took part in it. Asha was on the project to help her get her fitness back, but kids came there for all kinds of reasons. Some came because they were having problems at home, and others because they were having problems at school, but the one thing they all had in common was that they needed help. Working on the farm gave them something positive to focus on and helped them through their difficult times.

'Coming,' Asha called, as she hurried through the drizzly rain.

Inside, the barn was cosy and warm. Asha stood in

the doorway and breathed in the sweet smell of wood-smoke coming from the stove in the corner. The walls were covered with artwork done by children from local schools – a collage of paintings of the farm's small green paddocks, flower gardens and vegetable patches. There were lots of animal pictures too. Asha's favourite was a cute, lifelike drawing of Bubble and Squeak, the farm guinea pigs, with their golden fur and beady black eyes. There was also a cartoon-style picture of Rory where someone had given him extra-long, bendy legs and made his crazy white hair look like a huge cloud that had landed on his head.

'Asha – come into the warm,' Rory called, beckoning her over to the two big, comfy sofas next to the stove.

'I wish the farm was as bright and sunny as this right now,' Asha said, pointing to one of the colourful paintings on the wall. She took off her coat and hung it behind the door.

Rory smiled, causing his blue eyes to twinkle. 'Don't you worry. In a week or two you'll see a difference. It's almost Easter. Soon this place'll be a blaze of colour.'

'All right, Asha?'

Asha turned to see her friend Jack coming out of the storeroom, holding a football.

'Hi, Jack. What's the ball for?'

 15

'Cynthia,' Jack replied, looking slightly embarrassed.

'Cynthia the pig?' Asha exclaimed.

Over on the sofa, Rory chuckled. 'Jack's got a plan,' he told her. 'He reckons he can fix Cynthia's bad temper.'

Asha looked back at Jack questioningly.

Jack started rolling the ball about in his hands. 'I just thought that if she had something to kick about, it might help her not to be so grumpy.'

'That's brilliant!' Asha exclaimed, picturing the huge pig kicking the ball around her pen. 'Maybe she'll get really good at it and we can enter her into talent shows. She could be known as the Incredible Footballing Pig. People would come from all over the world to see her play. We could even—'

'All right, all right, let's not count our chickens,' Rory grinned. 'We haven't even shown her the ball yet. And knowing Cynthia, she'll find summat wrong with it. She probably prefers rugby,' he added with a chortle.

Asha smiled and went over to join Rory on the sofa. She still thought the football idea was a great one though. They'd tried just about everything else to cheer Cynthia up. And if anyone could get the crotchety rare-breed pig to like kicking a ball it was

Jack. Jack was on the Harvest Hope project because he'd been in trouble for fighting with some boys in his class who'd been bullying him. They'd been teasing Jack about his dyslexia, and the problems he had with reading and writing. But as far as Asha was concerned, Jack was one of the smartest people she knew.

Rory coughed loudly, which was his polite way of reminding them that they needed to get on with the meeting. Jack came and sat down on the sofa opposite them, still holding his football.

Asha looked around the barn for Kerry, the Harvest Hope co-ordinator.

Kerry was at her desk at the far end of the barn, talking into the telephone and twisting her long, black braids round her finger. Asha strained to try and hear what she was saying.

'Mr Jarvis, I understand, but I don't agree – local people love the farm.' Kerry was speaking very clearly and carefully, as she often did when Derrick Jarvis, finances manager of the local council, was on the phone.

Asha looked at Rory anxiously. Derrick Jarvis was always trying to find a reason to close the farm. He wanted to sell the land to a property developer to make money for the council. He just didn't seem to understand that some things were more important than money.

'Looks like Kerry's busy,' Rory said. 'So we'll have to carry on without her for the moment. First and foremost, we need to talk about Curly.'

'Oh, has it happened?' Asha sat up straight on the sofa in excitement. Curly was the farm's Dartmoor sheep, and she was about to give birth to a lamb.

'Not yet,' Rory replied. 'But it could be any day now. I've brought her into one of the stables so that we can keep an eye on her.'

'Can I do it?' Asha cried. 'I promise I'll check up on her all the time. I can keep her company so she doesn't feel scared. I bet she will feel a bit scared, won't she, as it's her first baby?'

'She probably will be feeling a bit out of sorts right now,' Rory replied with a nod.

'I could tell her stories,' Asha said. 'I used to love it when my mum told me stories when I was in hospital. It might help take her mind off it.'

Rory grinned at her. 'Aye, lass, I'm sure it would, the stories you tell. I want you and Jack to take responsibility for exercising her too. She needs regular walks to keep her fit and healthy for the birth. No football though,' he added, winking at Jack. 'Least, not till after she's had the baby!'

Jack laughed. 'Yep, no problem.'

'Thanks, Jack.' Rory looked pleased. 'I know you've had plenty of experience of lambs being born.'

Jack nodded and smiled. 'Yes, loads. Once, me and Grandad delivered five in one night!'

'You were so lucky, actually living on a real farm!' Asha exclaimed. 'I can't wait till the lamb arrives. How much longer do you think it will it be?'

Before Rory could answer there was a loud clatter from the other end of the barn as Kerry slammed the phone down. Then she got up and marched over to them, plonking herself down on the sofa next to Jack.

'That man!' she exclaimed. The silver bangles on her wrists jangled as she threw her arms up in despair.

Sitting next to her on the sofa, Jack kept quiet. He hated it when Mr Jarvis phoned up. It always meant trouble, and Jack didn't know what he'd do if anything happened to City Farm.

'He won't be able to close the farm down, will he?' Asha asked anxiously, as if reading Jack's mind.

Kerry shook her head. 'No, there's nothing to worry about. He was just being his usual difficult self.'

But Jack wasn't so sure. Nothing was safe when it came to farms. He knew that from what had happened to his grandad. When the old man had got too weak to do heavy work, he had to leave Hilltop, the farm where he'd lived his whole life. He'd had to leave all the animals too. And so had Jack and his mum.

Kerry grinned at Jack and Asha. 'Mr Jarvis did have one good piece of news for us though. Curly's baby lamb isn't going to be the only new arrival at the farm this Easter. Someone's going to join us at Harvest Hope for the holidays!'

'Yay!' Asha gave a whoop of excitement. 'Who is it?'

Jack looked down at his football in silence.

'You OK, Jack?' Kerry asked.

'Yup.'

But Jack wasn't OK. His chest felt tight, and his heart was pounding.

What if the new kid was one of the boys from his school? What if one of the bullies who'd called him a thicko had got excluded, and been sent here too?

'She's called Emily,' Kerry continued. 'She moved to the city recently and has been having a difficult time fitting in at her new school. They've asked if she can spend the Easter holidays with us, working on the farm.'

Jack breathed a sigh of relief. So the new arrival

would be a girl. That wouldn't be so bad. After all, Asha was great. He'd never met anyone who cared about animals as much as she did.

'Cool! I can't wait to show her round!' Asha said, her eyes shining with excitement. 'I'll never forget my first day here. It was so amazing to see the paddock and the flower garden and all of the animals – especially after so long in hospital.' A dreamy smile crept across Asha's face. 'The best bit was when I first saw Bubble and Squeak and they twitched their little noses at me. Or maybe it was when Stanley nuzzled me after I gave him a sugar cube.' She frowned. 'No, I think the very best bit was when I fed the chickens for the first time. No, it wasn't, it was when I found my first egg. That was amazing. It was still warm! Oh, but then there were the baby ducklings. They were so—'

'Yes, yes, we get the picture,' Rory interrupted with a smile.

Jack couldn't help smiling too. Once Asha got going it was very hard to get her to stop.

'Well anyway, it was the best day of my life,' Asha said.

'I hope Emily doesn't talk quite as much as you, Asha, or none of us will be able to get a word in edgeways,' Kerry teased.

Asha grinned. 'I can't help it. There's always so much to say!'

There was a clang outside as the gates opened. Jack heard the purr of a car coming into the yard. He went over to the window and looked out through the rain-speckled glass. The new girl had arrived.

Jack watched as she got out of the car, dragging her bag behind her. She looked a bit older than him, with soft, wavy brown hair.

But there was nothing soft about the girl's face. There was a cross look in her eyes and her lips were pursed together tightly. Jack sighed. He knew that girls could be bullies too, and after all of the hassle he'd had at school the last thing he wanted was any trouble at the farm.

'She's here! She's here!' Asha cried, joining him by the window. 'Ooh, this is going to be so much fun.'

'Jack, can you pop to the café and get some cakes?' Kerry asked as she walked over to the door.

Jack nodded. Maybe one of the home-made cakes from the café would cheer the new girl up – they always brought a smile to Asha's face. But as he watched the girl stomping towards them across the yard, he couldn't help thinking it would take a lot more than a flapjack to make her happy.

Chapter Two

'Quick, love, before you get soaked,' Emily's dad called over his shoulder.

Emily shuddered as cold raindrops hit her face. It was good to be out of the car though. Denise was always scrubbing the seats with antiseptic wipes, but there was still a whiff of milk and baby sick around Leon's baby carrier.

Her dad had parked the car by a ramshackle building covered with wooden beams and a lopsided, red-tiled roof. It looked like it had been there for hundreds of years. Over the door was a sign in bright yellow letters. Emily read the words: *HARVEST HOPE PROJECT*. She sighed. If they *hoped* they were going to make her enjoy going to school they were going to be disappointed.

She looked around for some farm animals – cows or sheep or horses – but all she could see were groups of visitors trudging about under umbrellas. There were families with little kids and even a couple of old-age pensioners all wandering around in the cold and rain actually looking happy to be there.

'Hi, you must be Emily. And you must be Mr Keane?' A black woman with silver beads in her plaited hair called to them from the door of the building. A thin Asian girl was standing next to her, smiling. Emily looked down at the puddle-covered ground, wishing that her cheeks didn't have to go red every time she met someone new.

'Yes, and you must be Kerry,' Emily's dad said in his cheery everything's-just-fine voice. The one he used when everything was anything *but* fine. He walked over to the woman and shook her hand.

She looked more like a pop star than someone who worked on a farm, Emily thought, glancing at Kerry's bright red lipstick and leopard-spotted wellingtons. Or she would have done if she wasn't wearing a dirty, baggy body-warmer.

'Come in, come in,' Kerry said, beckoning to them.

Emily trudged after her dad into the building.

A tall older man came over to greet them as soon

as they entered. He had snowy white hair and broad shoulders, and his red face looked as if he spent most of his time outdoors.

'Welcome to City Farm,' he said, smiling at Emily. 'I'm Rory, the farm manager. I expect you'll be wanting to get outside and see the animals.'

'Not really,' Emily replied.

Rory looked surprised and Emily's dad frowned.

'Sorry,' he said quickly. 'Emily seems to have forgotten her manners.'

Emily instantly felt bad. She hadn't meant to be rude. It was just that she'd rather stay in the warm and find a corner where she could sit and read.

'Don't worry,' Kerry replied. 'It isn't the nicest day to be outside, is it, Emily? Now, I suppose the school told you all about the Harvest Hope project and what we do here?'

Emily nodded glumly. After the shame of running out of the Easter assembly she and her dad had been called in to go for a meeting with Miss Trimble.

'We think it might be a good idea for Emily to try spending some time at City Farm over the Easter holidays,' Miss Trimble had told her dad. 'They have an excellent project for children who are going through, you know, *problems.*'

She'd whispered the word 'problems' as if that would stop Emily from hearing it. But Emily did hear and she didn't understand – the only 'problem' she had was that her mum had died, and she'd had to come and live with her dad and Denise, who had no time for her because they were too busy with baby Leon. How was being sent to work on a farm going to help that? But her dad had nodded enthusiastically, as if he couldn't wait to get rid of her, and so here they were.

'Why don't you and I go and get the paperwork sorted, Mr Keane,' Kerry said, 'and we'll let Rory and the others show Emily around. We can go through health and safety later, Emily, but I'm sure you'd like a look round first.'

Emily's face went hot with embarrassment as she watched her dad follow Kerry to a desk at the far end of the room. How could he just dump her here with a bunch of strangers?

Because he wants you out of the way, a tight little voice in her head replied. *Just like Denise wants you out of the way, so they can play happy families with Leon.*

Emily felt someone nudge her arm. It was the skinny girl.

'Hi, I'm Asha,' she said. She was wearing a flowery

top over trousers, and a green woolly hat. 'Love your trainers! Are they new?'

Emily nodded. They were only a cheap pair from the bargain shoe shop. Denise wouldn't let her have the cool, sequinned All-Stars that she'd asked for. She said she didn't have enough money. She always seemed to have plenty of money to spend on toys and clothes for Leon though.

A door burst open on the other side of the room and Emily got a quick glimpse of a counter with a drinks machine, and people sitting at tables. The smell of coffee and freshly baked cookies wafted in as a young boy with freckles and sandy, sticking-up hair came walking through.

'Here, have a flapjack, Asha,' he said, passing her a plate. He offered one to Emily cautiously, but she shook her head. She felt too nervous to eat anything.

'Nice one, Jack,' Kerry called across. She turned back to Emily's dad. 'Asha gets so involved with everything that often she forgets to eat,' she explained. 'But Jack makes sure she doesn't miss out on her snacks. She's been a bit poorly – needs to keep her strength up.'

Mr Keane nodded. 'The work you do here is wonderful,' he said. 'It will do Emily so much good to be here.'

Emily felt her face growing hot again. Why was her dad talking about her like that? As if there was something *wrong* with her? She bit her lip and blinked back the tears that were stinging her eyes.

'Here!' Asha stuffed some flapjack into her mouth, and grabbed two green anoraks with the Harvest Hope logo on them. She gave one to Emily. 'You'd better get some wellingtons from the shelf by the door or your trainers will get ruined.'

Emily shrugged. 'I don't mind.'

'Try these.' The old man, Rory, took a pair down. They were green and splattered with dried mud. 'It's a good idea to wear proper footwear on the farm. Never know what you might tread in!'

Emily cringed as Rory let out a loud laugh. Reluctantly, she kicked off her trainers and pulled on the green wellingtons. She wondered how many other feet had been inside them before hers. And what horrible things they had trodden in.

'That's the way,' Rory said, smiling at her before turning to Asha and Jack. 'Now where shall we take Emily first?'

'Cynthia!' Jack said, right away.

Asha grinned. 'Yes! We can bring her the football.'

Emily watched as Jack went to collect a football from one of the sofas at the end of the room. What kind of animal was called Cynthia and liked playing football?

'We'll just finish up here – you guys go ahead,' Kerry called from her desk.

Emily's dad smiled at her nervously. 'OK, darling?' he asked, but Emily knew it wasn't really a question. She put on the green anorak and followed Jack, Asha and Rory out of the barn. It was still raining, but not quite so heavily.

'Who's Cynthia?' Emily mumbled as they walked down a wide gravel path behind the barn and away from the farmyard.

But nobody heard her. Asha was busy nattering away to Jack, and Rory was saying hello to a man with a beard, who was selling potted plants from a little stall in some kind of garden area.

Asha turned to Emily. 'Our volunteers plant bulbs in the flower garden and then we sell them when they've grown,' she explained. 'We're always looking for ways to make money for the farm.'

Emily looked at the garden. It was a bit higgledy-piggledy, with clusters of rose bushes and plants and flowers all competing for space, but she could see how it might look lovely in the summer. There was a little wooden bench tucked under an apple tree at the bottom of the garden. Emily imagined sitting there with one of her favourite books while the birds chirped all around her. She was about to ask Asha if they sold the apples from the tree too, but just then an old lady shuffled towards them, carrying a pot of crocuses.

'This is Miss James, Emily,' Rory said. 'She's one of our most regular visitors. All right, Miss James? Lovely weather, eh?'

The old lady smiled. 'Lovely weather if you're a duck,' she said with a chuckle. 'That's why I've bought these,' she said, waving the crocuses. 'Wonderful, aren't they? Such beautiful colours.'

Emily thought of how her mum had always filled their flat with crocuses the moment spring arrived. She pulled her hood down further over her face and carried on trudging along.

Next they came to a vegetable plot full of rows of runner beans. A scarecrow stood in the middle, with his stick arms outstretched.

'He's called Rory the Second,' Asha said.

Rory let out a bellowing laugh. 'Not quite got my good looks and charm though, eh?'

Jack and Asha laughed but Emily shivered. With his big hat and long black coat the scarecrow reminded her of one of the characters from her nightmares – the one who always came to take her mum away.

A moment later, they came to a low wall with a gate in it, which led into a straw-covered yard. On the other side of the yard was a shed.

Jack opened the gate, and went in. There was a rustling noise from inside the shed, and then a loud grunt as a huge, orange-coloured pig came out. The pig came trundling over to them and stood on her hind legs, resting her front feet on top of the wall. Her fierce little eyes glared at them. Emily flinched, scared that the pig would jump right over.

Jack came back over to the wall. 'Don't worry, she can't escape,' he said.

'I wasn't worried,' Emily retorted. She didn't want to look like she was scared. 'I didn't know pigs could be ginger,' she added, staring at Cynthia's orange hide.

Jack looked surprised, and Emily realized that his sandy hair was almost ginger. Maybe she'd upset him.

'Sorry, I didn't mean—' she began, but Rory interrupted.

'Cynthia's a Tamworth,' he said. 'They're always this colour.'

'Tamworths are the oldest variety of pig – directly descended from wild boars,' Jack added.

Cynthia started to grunt loudly. Emily took a step back but Asha smiled. 'Cynthia can be a bit grumpy, but she's really well-behaved with Jack,' she said. 'He knows just how to get round her. He's got a really cool present for her too. Shall we give it to her now?' Asha looked at Rory.

Rory glanced over at Emily. 'Why don't we let Jack take care of Cynthia while you and I take Emily to see our star attraction? I get the feeling pigs aren't exactly Emily's cup of tea – yet!'

'OK,' Asha replied cheerily before turning to Emily. 'Come on. You'll love our star attraction. It's brilliant!'

Emily sighed. So far she'd been expected to be excited about some potted plants and an orange pig. She wondered what the 'star attraction' might be. A pile of horse manure? A rusty old tractor?

Why had her dad dumped her here? After her parents had got divorced, Emily had always spent half of her holidays with her dad. He'd liked hanging out with her then, he'd always taken time off work and they'd done fun things together. But since she'd come to live with him and Denise full time, he always seemed too busy with Leon to spend any time with her. He was probably bored of her now that he saw her all the time.

Asha led her over to a stable, where the top half of the door was fastened open.

Emily peered into the darkness inside. She could just make out a sheep sitting on a bed of straw. 'Who's this?' she asked.

'It's Curly!' Asha announced grandly, as if she were introducing the Queen. She opened the bottom half of the door and gestured for Emily to come inside. Emily followed her slowly. She wasn't sure she wanted to get that close to the sheep, but at least it couldn't be as bad as the pig.

As she drew nearer the sheep sniffed at Emily's hand with her velvet nose, and blinked her golden-brown eyes.

'Well, would you look at that!' Rory exclaimed from the doorway. 'She likes you, Emily. That's because you approached her quietly and gently. She's normally dead shy with strangers.'

Emily felt a tiny stab of pride. 'Hi, Curly,' she murmured. At last somebody in this city liked her.

'She's pregnant,' Asha said, stroking Curly's head. 'Her lamb's going to be born any day now.'

'Oh,' Emily replied, her heart sinking. Now she was up so close she could see the sheep's tummy bulging out at the sides under her thick fleece of creamy curls. Once Curly had her baby she wouldn't want to be friends with Emily any more. Babies took up all of their parents' time, as she knew only too well.

'We'll take good care of her, don't you worry,' Rory said. 'Curly and her baby will be just fine.'

'I'm not worried,' Emily snapped.

No one said anything for a moment. Asha gazed at Emily with wide eyes.

Emily wished she would stop, it was making her feel even worse. 'What?' she asked crossly, turning away so that Asha wouldn't see her cheeks burning.

'Emily, could you just keep an eye on Curly for a minute while Asha and I go and get some feed from the stable next door?' Rory asked.

Emily nodded, grateful for the chance of some time on her own. She sat down on the straw in the corner of the stable and wrapped her arms round her knees. After a couple of minutes, a face peered over the stable door. It was her dad.

'I'm off now, love,' he said. 'This really is a great place, Em. Kerry's a lovely lady, very easy to talk to, you know, if you wanted to talk to her about –

anything.' He looked down at the stable floor. 'You're going to love working here during the holidays. Trust me.'

Emily didn't say anything. She kept her eyes fixed on the straw. She would never, ever trust him again. He had lied to her so many times. *You'll always be my favourite girl, Em ... Denise and I really like having you to live with us ... Just because you've got a new baby brother doesn't mean we don't love you, Emily.*

And the worst lie of all. *Your mum will be out of hospital and back home with you really soon.* Remembering it made Emily's head hurt, and her stomach feel tight.

'OK, then. I'll see you later.'

Her dad gave a little sigh, and then he left. Off home to Denise and Leon and their perfect little family. Leaving Emily here, all alone. A couple of hot tears slid down her face.

Curly came across and sniffed Emily's hair. Emily dropped her head on her knees, and let her tears soak into her jeans. She had never felt so miserable in all her life.

Chapter Three

'I can't wait until all of the flowers are out,' Asha said. 'Rory says that any day now this place will be full of colour. It's going to look so pretty, don't you think?'

'Hmm.' Emily plucked another weed from the ground. Asha had asked her to help tidy up the flower garden after they'd fed Curly. Now her back was aching and her fingernails were caked with mud.

Since when have farms had flower gardens? moaned a mean voice inside her head. *This isn't a proper farm at all.*

But at least she had a job to be getting on with. Hopefully it might make the time go a bit quicker. Emily wondered if she ought to try and say something to Asha, but the way she chattered on, it was hard to get a word in.

'I love flowers, don't you?' Asha chirped. 'When I was in hospital my mum brought me flowers every day. She said that—'

'I hate flowers,' Emily interrupted. 'They give people hay fever and when they die they go all shrivelled up and gross.' She immediately felt horrible, but she hadn't been able to help herself. It was one thing listening to Asha talk about how great the farm was, but there was no way Emily could listen to her talking about her mum.

Asha stopped weeding and stared at her. Emily noticed that her face was shiny with sweat, but she still hadn't taken her hat off. She wondered if it was anything to do with her illness. She looked back down at the weeds, feeling slightly ashamed. She knew Asha was only trying to be friendly, but what was the point? Emily was only going to be at the farm for two weeks and then they'd never see each other again. Just like she'd probably never see any of her old friends again.

Emily thought of her best friend Joanna and wondered what she was doing. Before, on a cold day like today, Emily's mum would have probably taken them both swimming. And afterwards they would have shared a bag of hot, salty chips. When Emily had last spoken to Joanna on the phone, Joanna had been all excited because she'd been invited to a sleepover at Claire's. Life was carrying on without her back in her old hometown, while here in the city, hers was grinding to a halt.

'Asha! Asha! Come and look at Cynthia!' Jack came running into the garden, his cheeks flushed with excitement. 'I've got her playing with the football.'

'Do you want to come?' Asha asked Emily hesitantly.

Emily nodded. Although she didn't really fancy going back to see the pig, if she refused she would look even more unfriendly.

As they approached Cynthia's sty, the huge pig came blundering towards them. Emily made sure she stood well back from the wall this time. Cynthia was a whole lot bigger than her, and her little piggy eyes looked even more unfriendly than before.

'Hey, Cynth!' Jack called, running into the yard bouncing the football. Then he tossed it to the pig.

Asha clapped and cheered as Cynthia trundled the football around the straw-strewn ground.

'I'm going to try and train her to kick it through the door to her shed to score a goal,' Jack explained.

'Yay!' Asha cried, jumping up and down like a demented football fan. 'That'll be brilliant!'

For a moment, the image of the huge orange pig

playing football made Emily want to laugh and cheer too. But something stopped her – the same thing that had stopped her being friendly to Asha in the garden. There was no point. Once again she felt tears pricking her eyes.

'I'm going to wash my hands,' she muttered and she quickly turned and walked up the path to the farmyard. When she got there she saw a battered old van pull in. There was a big logo on the side with the words *Canine Rescue Centre* and an image of a Labrador puppy with its head on one side.

A man wearing brown overalls got out of the van. 'Hello, love, is the boss about?' he asked.

Before Emily could answer Rory emerged from the barn.

'All right, Mr Trent,' the man said. 'I've brought your new resident.'

'Morning, Dave.' Rory called. 'Let's take a look at her then.' He went round to the back of the van and waited as the man climbed inside, then came out holding a lead. On the other end was a black and white dog with a long, feathery tail. The dog was shivering, and her fur was matted and dirty. She looked up at Emily with big, scared eyes. *She'd be quite pretty, if she was washed and brushed*, Emily thought.

'Got a bit of collie in her, I reckon,' the man said. 'Just what you need on the farm.'

Rory bent down and reached his hand out, but the dog crouched down flat to the ground, as far away from him as she could get.

'Good job you could take her,' the man went on. 'We're full up, and no one wants to give a home to a nervous dog like Patch here.'

Emily felt a pang of sorrow. She knew only too well how it felt not to be wanted.

Rory stood up and Patch wriggled even further away, until she was hiding under the back of the van.

'No problem, Dave, she's welcome here. Come on, Patch.' Rory took the lead from the man and tried to pull the dog towards him. But she stayed under the van.

Good for you, Patch, Emily thought. If only she'd done the same thing that morning when her dad had come banging on her door to take her to the farm. If she'd lain on the carpet and refused to move, he would have had to leave her there.

Rory frowned. 'I'll go and get some doggy treats. See if I can coax her out.' He went to pass the lead back to Dave, but somehow it slipped out of his hand. Quick as a flash, Patch shot out from under the van and bolted across the yard, disappearing behind the stables.

'Wow. Go, Patch!' Emily whispered. She wished she could run like that. Sprint across the yard, dodge out between the open gates and never have to come back to the farm ever again.

'Don't worry, mate, you get on,' Rory said to Dave. 'We'll find her.'

'Are you sure?' Dave asked.

Rory smiled at him reassuringly. 'Yes. The farm's all fenced in. As long as we keep the gates shut she won't come to any harm. She just needs a bit of time to get used to the place, that's all.'

Emily and Rory watched as Dave got back into his van and backed it out of the gates.

When he had gone, Rory quickly closed the gates behind him and looked at Emily. 'It was really daft of me, letting go of her like that. Will you help me find her?'

Emily nodded.

'She needs help,' Rory continued gravely. 'I think the poor mite's had a very tough time.'

'Why?'

'Well, Dave says she was found running around the council estate, scavenging from the dustbins, no collar

41

on her. She must've been dumped.'

Emily shuddered as she pictured Patch, hungry and scared and all alone. 'Who would do that?'

Rory frowned. 'It happens all the time. People think it would be really nice to get a little puppy for a pet. Then they get bored with feeding and cleaning up after it, and taking it for walks. So they chuck it out.'

Emily couldn't help wondering whether her dad was feeling the same way about her. Maybe that was why he'd enrolled her on the Harvest Hope project, to try and get rid of her for a while.

'We need to find her as soon as we can,' Rory continued. 'She's so fearful I reckon she's been very badly treated. And she'll be very hungry and thirsty.'

Emily's eyes felt hot with tears. She wondered what could have happened to Patch to make her so scared.

'Maybe if we had some dog biscuits she might come out?' she suggested, looking at her feet, so that Rory couldn't see she was nearly crying.

'That's a great idea,' Rory replied. 'There's some in the blue cupboard in the barn. Why don't you go and fetch them and I'll go and see if I can find her.'

Emily nodded. She rushed into the barn, stuffed her pockets full of the bone-shaped biscuits and then ran back to join Rory at the stables.

 42

'No sign of her,' Rory said with a sigh.

'Patch?' Emily called, straining her eyes for a glimpse of the dog's black and white coat in a dark corner. But there was nothing to be seen.

Emily remembered the look of terror in the dog's eyes and how she had been shivering. 'Patch? Please, come out!'

But no matter how hard Emily and Rory looked there was no answering bark, no rustle from the undergrowth. Not even the gleam of a wary eye from the thick hedges that surrounded the paddocks at the bottom of the farm. Patch was nowhere to seen. It was as if the sad little black and white dog had never existed.

Chapter Four

Emily stood outside her dad's house and watched as Kerry's car drove off down the road. Her hands were so cold after the long afternoon of hunting for Patch that she could hardly feel her fingers and her key was hiding somewhere in the bottom of her bag. She gave up trying to find it and pressed the doorbell. No one answered.

Emily stamped her feet to keep warm, and thought of the dog, still hiding outside in the chilly rain. Even though Jack and Asha and Kerry had all joined in the search, it had been no good. Patch clearly didn't want to be discovered.

If only they could have found her before it was time to leave. Rory had looked so sad as he stood under the big tree by the duck pond and told them it was time to call it a day.

'She'll come out when she's hungry,' Kerry had said in the car on the way home. But Emily wasn't so sure.

She pressed the bell a second time, but still no one came. The light was on in the sitting room, so Denise must be at home. Maybe she was upstairs.

Suddenly the door flew open. Denise stood in the doorway in her dressing gown, carrying baby Leon on her hip. Her hair was scraped back into a ponytail and her eyes looked puffy and tired.

'Oh, hello, Emily. Where's your key?'

'It's in my bag somewhere but I couldn't find it,' Emily began to explain, but Denise had already turned around and was trudging back along the hall.

Emily followed her through to the kitchen. Denise sat down at the table with Leon on her lap. She picked up a feeding bottle and tried to put it in the baby's mouth. He turned his head away.

'Come on, you wanted it a minute ago,' Denise said, waving the bottle at him. Leon pulled a face and started to cry. Denise sighed loudly.

'What's for tea?' Emily asked.

'There's some leftover pasta from last night,' Denise muttered. 'You can heat it up in the microwave.' She turned back to Leon and stroked his little quiff of blond hair. 'I suppose I'd better give my lovely boy his bath then, hadn't I, if he doesn't want any more supper!' she cooed. It was as if she had two different voices – a grumpy, tired one for Emily and a soppy baby one for Leon. Emily didn't know which one she hated the most.

She watched as Denise left the room. The back of her dressing gown shoulder was stained white with Leon's sicked-up milk. Emily shut her eyes and imagined that she was back at home, in the lovely flat with the big windows and the high ceilings where she and her mum used to live. It was on the top floor of a large Victorian house, and you could look out from the living room into the branches of the tall trees in the old garden. When she was little, Emily and her mum had pretended that they actually lived in a treetop, in the middle of an enchanted forest. They would snuggle up on the sofa together and her mum would tell her stories about all the magical creatures that lived in the other trees.

But it was no use remembering how things used to be. It just made how they were now feel even worse. Emily opened her eyes and went to put the pasta into the microwave. Then she sat down at the table. As usual it was cluttered with Leon's things.

Emily frowned. There was barely any room for her to have her dinner. The table was a sea of bottles and bottle warmers and dummies and sterilizing wipes and a pile of baby vests and a pack of nappies. And that wasn't even counting the stupid toys. Although he was tiny, Leon had taken over the whole house.

Emily pushed a fluffy teddy and a purple plastic dinosaur out of the way so that she would have room for her plate. Then she heard the front door click open. Her dad was home from work.

'How did it go, Em?' he asked, as he entered the room and added his briefcase and a crumpled-up newspaper to all the mess on the table. 'Good day?'

'It was OK,' Emily replied.

'Great!' Her dad looked at the cluttered table, then he sighed and took off his glasses to rub the top of his nose.

'Someone brought a dog to the farm...' Emily began. She really wanted to tell her dad about Patch.

'That's nice,' he said, smiling at Emily and blinking because he couldn't see very well without his glasses.

'No, it was awful, because—'

There was a loud roar from upstairs. Leon obviously wasn't happy about being bathed. Mr Keane's face crumpled into a frown.

'Waaaah! WAAAH!' Leon's shrieks were ear-splitting, even from all the way upstairs.

'—we lost her,' Emily continued.

'Jonathan?' Denise shouted down the stairs. 'Can you come up here? I need a hand giving Leon his bath.'

'Coming!' Emily's dad got up and put his glasses back on. 'Sorry, love,' he said as he rushed from the room. 'Tell me another time, eh?'

Emily shook her head and sighed. It was always like this now. Even when they were alone together, her dad didn't listen to her. It wasn't just the house that Leon had taken over, it was her dad, as well.

On the way home from the farm Kerry had given Emily an exercise book. 'I'd like you to keep a diary while you're at City Farm,' she had said. 'Sometimes, when you've been through a bad time, it can really helpful to write about how you are feeling.' But Emily didn't want to write about how lonely and sad she felt – it would only make her feel even worse.

She swallowed back the tears that were threatening to break loose and pour down her face. She tried to clear some more space on the table and accidentally knocked a cardboard book onto the floor. It fell open at a picture of a black and white cow, and made a silly moo-ing noise.

'Stupid thing!' Emily hissed. She picked the book up and threw it at the wall. 'That'll shut you up!' she said, as it gave a final, wobbly 'moo-oo' and went quiet.

The purple dinosaur lay on the table, grinning up at her. Something about its sharp-toothed, lop-sided smile reminded her of Cynthia the pig. She grabbed it and hurled it at the dishes that were piled in the sink. Emily felt a lot better as she watched it tumble headfirst into the scummy water.

Then she noticed that the teddy was staring at her with its bulging eyes. It looked a bit nervous, as if it was frightened of that big, bad, scary girl, Emily Keane. It reminded her of the way Asha had stared at her when she'd told her she hated flowers. She picked up the teddy and chucked it at the sink too. It hit the dirty plates with a crash.

'Emily!'

She spun round to see her dad standing in the doorway.

'What are you doing? That's Leon's favourite toy!' He went over to the sink and rescued the teddy, smoothing down its fur.

Emily's heart was beating fast, and her head felt as

if it might burst.

'Leon, Leon! It's always Leon!' she said. 'You never think about anything except that stupid baby.'

Her dad's face turned red. He took a deep breath, as if he were trying to keep calm. 'That's not true. And how can you talk about him like that? He's your little brother.'

'He's a little monster!' Emily was so mad her legs were trembling. She knew she shouldn't speak to her dad like this, but now she had started, the words just kept pouring out. 'I hate him!' she yelled. 'I wish he'd never been born!'

'Stop it, Emily,' her dad said through gritted teeth. 'Be quiet.'

'Why should I? All Leon ever does is scream. Why should I have to shut up when he won't?'

'Because I will not have you behaving like this at home, I—'

'Home?' Emily interrupted. 'This isn't my home. I hate it here!'

Mr Keane's mouth fell open. Then he shouted at the top of his voice: 'That is *ENOUGH*, Emily! Go to your room. *NOW!*'

Emily had never heard him shout before. Her whole body was shaking, but somehow she made her

way upstairs. Her dad must hate her, to yell at her like that. He must really, really hate her.

But this little house *wasn't* her home. Her home was with her mum, in the lovely, clean, quiet flat with the windows that looked out over the trees in the garden.

Emily lay face down on her bed. Through the thin bedroom wall, she could hear Leon still screaming, on and on.

'Oh, Mum,' she whispered, 'why did you have to die?'

The tears she'd been holding back slid out of her eyes and soaked into her pillow.

Chapter Five

Mr Keane stopped the car outside the big gates of the farm and turned to face Emily.

'Are you OK?' he asked, for about the fifth time that morning.

Emily nodded, even though she felt far from OK. Her head ached and her eyes felt sore. She wished she was really little again and could just crawl onto his lap for a hug. She felt so bad about the way she had shouted at him the night before. Emily glanced across at her dad. Maybe if she just told him how she was feeling he might actually listen to her …

'Right then, I'd better get off,' he said, looking back at the road. 'I promised Denise I'd take her and Leon to the baby clinic.'

Emily sighed and undid her seat belt. There was

no point even trying. All he ever thought about was Leon. 'OK. See you later.'

As she trudged into the farmyard she saw Jack and Asha standing outside the barn. Asha wasn't wearing her hat today. Instead, her hair was covered with a bright pink scarf.

'Hi, Emily!' she called. 'We've got a really cool job for you today.'

'I think you'll like it more than going to see Cynthia,' Jack added. 'It's kind of more of a girly thing to do.'

Emily felt anger prickling beneath her skin. What did he mean by that? Was he trying to say that girls weren't as good as boys?

'I'm not scared of Cynthia, if that's what you're saying,' she replied crossly. 'I just don't like pigs.'

'Well, this *is* a farm,' Jack said. 'I'm afraid you're always going to get pigs on a farm.' He looked at Asha and grinned.

Great, now they were making fun of her. Well, Emily didn't care one bit. It wasn't as if she'd chosen to come here. The only thing she cared about in the stupid place was Patch. Emily looked over at the stables, hoping for a glimpse of her.

Just then Rory emerged from the barn. He was holding a large pail.

'Ah, young Miss Keane,' he boomed.

'Hello,' Emily muttered. 'Is Patch OK? Did you find her?'

''Fraid not.' Rory answered. 'But don't worry. We've kept the gates locked so she won't have gone far. I'm sure she'll show her face when she's hungry enough. Has Asha told you the plan for today?'

Emily shook her head. Where could Patch be? Had she really found a hiding place on the farm, or had she somehow managed to slip out and escaped to somewhere else, far away? She wondered if she'd ever see the frightened, black and white dog again.

'We're going to sort out Curly's stable,' Asha said excitedly. 'Get it all nice and clean and then we're going to clip her wool so she's ready for her lamb to be born! We thought you'd like to do that.'

Emily glared at her. Did everything always have to be about babies?

'Why?' she snapped.

Asha looked back at her blankly, the smile rapidly fading from her face. 'Why what?'

'Why would you think I'd like to do that? I'm not interested in stupid babies.'

Asha looked down at the ground. Jack glared at Emily. Emily glared back. It was just like the night before in the kitchen. All of the anger inside of Emily was spilling out and she didn't know how to stop it.

'All right, all right,' Rory said. 'Why don't I show Emily the chicken shed while you two make a start on Curly's stable?'

'Yes, come on, Asha,' Jack said, taking her by the arm. 'Let's get out of here.'

'She hates me,' Asha said as she and Jack headed over to Curly's stable.

'Who hates you?'

They both turned to see Kerry standing behind them.

'Emily,' Asha muttered. 'No matter how hard I try, she just doesn't want to be friends.'

Kerry put her arm round Asha. 'Are you OK, honey?'

Asha nodded, but she actually felt quite shaky.

'It's not you, Asha – you aren't doing anything wrong,' Kerry said. 'It's just that Emily's having a very tough time right now, and she doesn't know how to cope with it. That's why she's lashing out at anyone who comes near her.'

'I don't care if she's having a bad time,' Jack retorted. 'It's no excuse for being so rude.'

'Give her a chance, Jack,' Kerry said. 'It is only her second day.'

'I did give her a chance,' Jack said. 'I thought if she helped us with Curly this morning, we could get talking and maybe make friends. But she bit my head off when I asked her. And yesterday she just walked away when Cynthia was playing with the football. Like she thought it was really silly. And she was really mean to Asha just now. Who wants to be friends with someone like that?'

Kerry thought for a moment. Then she looked at Jack. 'Do you remember how grumpy you were, when you first came here?' she asked.

Jack frowned as he thought back to his first days at the farm. How small and cramped it had seemed after his grandad's place. Just one cow and a few sheep. And how silly he'd thought the little paddocks were, after the wide acres of Hilltop Farm.

He remembered too how suspicious he'd been of everyone, even Asha. How he'd waited for her to sneer at him for not being able to read very well. And he winced as he recalled what he'd said about her favourite animals, the guinea pigs. *'They're just boring little pets! You wouldn't find them on a proper farm.'* He hadn't thought that it might have hurt Asha's feelings.

'OK,' he said, after a long pause. 'Maybe you're right.'

Kerry nodded. 'Be a little patient. It's only Emily's second day. I'll be having a chat with her later. But in the meantime, give her a chance.'

'I'll try,' Jack replied. 'But she'd better not be mean to Asha again.'

Emily looked around at the big shed where the hens lived. They could go outside and run around in their wire enclosure if they wanted, but most of them were sitting inside today, fluffing up their feathers and clucking cheerily to each other.

'Why are these ones kept in here?' she asked, thinking of the other chickens that always seemed to be pecking around by the stables.

'These are the laying hens,' Rory told her. 'We keep them in the shed so it's easy to find the eggs. I'll clean out their food and water containers. Maybe you'd like to have a go at egg collecting.' He held out a cardboard egg tray.

There was a row of big boxes all along one wall, where the hens had their nests, and Emily had to reach down inside them for the eggs. The nests were lined with hay and felt warm and cosy against her cold fingers. They reminded her of the comfy duvet on her mum's big bed, where she used to cuddle up on Sunday mornings and read. She snuggled her hand down into the soft hay and closed her eyes for a moment, so she could remember better.

'All right?' Rory's voice interrupted her daydream.

Emily quickly opened her eyes, and nodded.

'I'm just going to check up on the others, see how they're doing with Curly,' he told her. 'There's a sack of corn over there, if you wouldn't mind filling up the food containers.' Then he went, leaving her alone with the hens.

Emily worked her way along the row of nests, filling up the tray. As she worked, she couldn't help thinking of Asha and how hurt she'd looked when she'd shouted at her. She sighed and put the last two eggs in the tray. Then she put the tray on a shelf by the door and went over to the sack. As she picked up the scoop to ladle out the corn, Emily heard something.

It didn't sound like one of the chickens. And it seemed to be coming from under her feet. She bent down and listened. There it was again. A thin, high, whining sound.

Emily went outside. The shed was raised up off the ground on thick wooden posts. She looked into the dark space underneath and saw two bright eyes glowing up at her. The squeaky, whining noise came again.

'Patch!' she whispered. Now she could see the dog's black and white fur, all tangled and dirty.

She remembered how Patch had fled from Rory, dashing across the farmyard. But the dog showed no sign of running away now. Perhaps she realized that Emily didn't want to hurt her, or yell at her. Emily crouched right down and stayed very still, peering under the shed. After a moment, she stretched out her hand. She touched the dog's wet, cold fur and felt her thin body shivering with fear.

Patch must have been hiding under here all night, in the cold. And she was clearly much too frightened to come out. What bad things had been done to her, to make her so afraid of human beings?

'It's OK, don't be scared,' Emily whispered. 'No one's going to be cruel to you any more. I won't let them.' She heard the dog whimpering again. 'Don't cry. I won't tell anyone you're here. It's all right.'

Emily stood up. There was no one about. If she was really quick, she could fetch some food and water and a warm blanket, without anyone seeing her.

'Wait there, Patch,' she whispered. 'I'll be right

back, don't worry. You're going to be all right!'

Emily jumped up and raced along the winding path back to the farmyard. She was in such a hurry she didn't notice Rory watching her from the other side of the chicken shed, a beaming smile upon his face.

Chapter Six

Emily tiptoed up to the barn and peered in through the window. Inside, she could see the big sofa with lots of woollen blankets tossed over it. She remembered how cosy those blankets were. One of them would make a perfect nest for Patch to sleep on.

Over in the office area of the barn, Kerry was sitting at her desk, talking on the phone.

Don't go in! a little voice whispered inside Emily's head. *She'll see you and she'll ask why you're taking the blanket. You can't tell her. No one must know about Patch. If they come to see her she might get scared and run away again.*

From the other side of the yard, Stanley the pony neighed to Emily and banged on the stable door with his hoof.

'What's up?' She went over to pat him. He blew

 61

down his nose at her, his warm breath smelling of sweet hay.

Stanley was wearing a bright green rug today. The edge of a warm, fleecy lining showed where the rug fitted around his neck.

'You look great,' Emily told him. 'I bet you're as snug as a bug in that rug!'

Stanley wiggled his top lip as if he was laughing. Then he nudged her with his nose, hoping for a sugar lump.

Emily grinned. 'Sorry, I haven't got anything for you.'

Seeing the pony in his rug had given Emily an idea. She gave Stanley a final pat, and went to look over the door of the old stable next to his. This was used as a storeroom. All the saddles and bridles and brushes for the horses and ponies were kept there, as well as some big bins of animal food.

The saddles were all resting on brackets that came out from the wall, and the bridles were hanging neatly, each on its own hook. Emily noticed something made of blue fabric lying in a heap in the corner.

She went into the stable to have a closer look. It was a blue horse rug, just like Stanley's green one. Just the thing for making a warm, comfy dog bed.

Patch would need something to eat too. Emily lifted the lid of the biggest food bin. It was full of corn, no use for a dog at all. She tried another, smaller bin. Inside was a paper sack containing round pellets. They smelled meaty, like dog food. Emily checked the side of the bag and saw a picture of a black and white collie, with a pink lolling tongue.

'Perfect!' she said to herself, as she stuffed several handfuls of the pellets into her coat pockets.

Next to the bins was a stack of metal food bowls. Emily helped herself to two of them. One for food and one for water. Then she picked up the rug and tried to tuck it under her arm. It was too big and heavy, and it kept slipping down. She'd never be able to carry it to the chicken shed.

Luckily someone had parked a wheelbarrow inside the stable. It had a few strands of dirty straw in the bottom of it.

Why is everything on this farm so messy? Emily thought, as she found a tissue in her pocket and wiped it clean. Then she folded up the rug and popped it into the barrow, with the two metal bowls on top.

The wheelbarrow was very heavy with the rug inside. It pulled on her arms as she trundled it across the farmyard.

'Emily!' Kerry's voice called from the barn door.

Emily stopped in her tracks, her heart beating fast. How was she going to explain what she was doing with the wheelbarrow and the horse rug?

But Kerry didn't look suspicious. 'Are you taking that for Curly?' she asked.

Emily nodded. She didn't want to lie to Kerry. Maybe just keeping quiet and not saying anything wasn't quite so bad as fibbing.

Kerry smiled. 'Can you come straight back after? I need your help with something.'

'Sure!' Emily spluttered.

She hurried away, shoving the barrow along the path so fast that she was out of breath by the time she got to the chicken shed.

'Phew! I'm glad that's over.' She pushed the barrow right up next to the shed. 'Patch!' she called, peering underneath. 'It's me – I'm back!'

For a second she thought the dog had gone. She couldn't see her anywhere in the darkness. Then she saw the flash of Patch's eyes. She was crouching down right at the back, shivering, with her ears pressed flat against her head. She looked terrified.

'Patch! I didn't mean to scare you. It's just an old wheelbarrow. I used it to carry all the things I've brought you,' Emily explained, speaking gently to reassure her.

Patch's ears pricked up and she gave a little whine. Emily soothed her some more, and then she got the horse rug out of the barrow and started dragging it under the shed.

It was hard work. Emily had to crawl right underneath and pull the heavy rug after her, stopping every few seconds to talk to Patch so she wouldn't be too frightened.

At last she managed to get it right into the corner. She folded it, fleecy side up so it would be soft and cosy to lie on. Patch lay still and watched her with bright eyes.

'There! Now you'll be warm and dry when you go to sleep,' Emily said. Then she wriggled back out and emptied the dog food from her pockets into one of the metal bowls and filled the other one with fresh water from the butt at the side of the shed. She pushed both the bowls underneath.

Patch was creeping over to have a drink when Emily heard the distant sound of Kerry's voice calling her.

'Emily? Where've you got to?'

She reached under to stroke the dog. 'I've got to go now but I'll come back soon. At least you won't have

 65

to lie on the ground any more. And there's plenty for you to eat and drink.'

Emily felt Patch's warm tongue lick her fingers, and then she had to run. Kerry was calling her again.

'I love it when the daffs start coming,' Kerry said, looking around at the daffodils that were flowering under the trees near the duck pond. 'Lots of them are still just buds, but there's enough flowers out already to really brighten up the barn. Thanks for helping me pick them.'

Kerry had already collected a big bunch. Emily had only managed to pick two before her eyes clouded with tears. The daffodil flowers that were open looked like yellow faces nodding in the sunshine. They reminded Emily of that morning at assembly, when she was supposed to recite the daffodil poem. The morning everything had gone so badly wrong.

'So, it's your second day here,' Kerry said. 'How're you feeling?'

Emily shrugged. She pulled at the stem of another daffodil and added it to her two. She wondered what Patch was doing. Was she eating the food now, or maybe curling up on her new bed?

'Did you write in your diary?' Kerry asked.

Emily shook her head.

Kerry squatted down to pick more daffodils. She looked up at Emily. 'If you're hurting or you're angry and you write about it, it can really help. Sometimes it's easier to write than talk.'

Emily stared at the flowers in her hand. They were so bright, so perfect, like little suns with their yellow petals. They'd die so quickly, now she'd snapped their stems.

'You can write anything and it's just between you and the diary. No one will answer you back, or tell you you're wrong.'

'I hate picking flowers,' Emily said.

Once, when her mum was in hospital, Emily had picked some flowers from the garden to give to her. The nurse put them in water, but next time Emily visited their petals had all turned brown and they were hanging down over the side of the vase. It was very hot in the ward where her mum was.

'Why d'you hate it?' Kerry smiled at her.

Emily looked down at the floor. 'They die so quickly, once you've picked them. It makes me sad.'

Kerry nodded. 'I know what you mean. But the weather forecast said it would get windy later. I thought we could bring the daffodils inside so they wouldn't get spoiled.'

Emily hadn't thought of that. Maybe it *was* better to have the flowers in the barn rather than leave them to get all battered and knocked down by the wind. She picked another couple to add to her three, and then she gave them to Kerry.

Kerry thanked her. Then she said: 'Feelings are very powerful things, Emily. They can take us over.'

'What d'you mean?'

'An emotion like anger or sadness can be so strong that sometimes it makes you forget who you are. And sometimes it can make you forget about other people too. It can make you be not very thoughtful towards them.'

Emily's face felt hot. *Kerry's talking about me*, she thought. *About how nasty I was to Asha. She's right. I was feeling so miserable, I didn't think about Asha at all.*

Kerry stood up. 'Let's take these in and put them in some water.'

'I'm sorry if I was rude,' Emily said. 'I bet Asha hates me.'

Kerry shook her head. 'She doesn't hate you at all, but she is a bit upset. It would be good if you could apologize to her.'

'All right.' Emily felt quite shaky at the thought of

it. But Asha had tried really hard to be friendly. She didn't deserve to be upset. It wasn't her fault if Emily was miserable.

They started walking back to the farmyard, Kerry carrying a whole armful of the bright yellow daffodils.

'Have a go at writing in your diary tonight,' she said. 'You could write about the farm. Or your new school. Or maybe you'd want to write about your baby brother.'

'Half-brother,' Emily said quickly.

'Whatever you feel, just write it all down.' Kerry paused. Then she said, 'You could even write about your mum.'

Emily didn't say anything. She didn't want to write in the diary. What was the point of it? It wouldn't make things any better. It wouldn't bring her mum back, or make baby Leon disappear. It wouldn't make the kids at her new school be nicer to her.

After Emily helped Kerry put the daffodils into vases they went to the stable to find the others.

Curly was sitting up on her large, woolly bottom. Jack was standing behind her, holding onto her front legs to keep her still. Asha was tickling the ewe under the chin and telling her to relax, the shearing would soon be over.

Rory was snipping at Curly's wool with a pair of shears that looked like scissors with sharp, triangular blades. As he snipped, the ewe's cream-coloured curls were peeling away from her body in one big fleece. Curly's skin was very white and smooth without her wool.

'Doesn't that hurt?' Emily asked.

'We're only shearing her,' Jack said. 'It doesn't hurt at all. She could keep her fleece if she lived outside. But she's going to give birth in the stable. Her coat needs to be clean and smooth, all ready for the baby lamb. That's right, isn't it, Asha?'

Emily flinched. She wished Asha would say something, but she didn't even look at Emily. She just carried on tickling Curly's chin.

Emily turned to Kerry, speaking quietly so no one else could hear. 'What should I do? Shall I say sorry now?'

Kerry shook her head. 'Maybe wait till they've finished.'

Jack and Asha were whispering together, and Asha was grinning.

I bet they're making fun of me, Emily thought, *because I didn't understand about the shearing.* Her face burned with embarrassment.

Rory looked up. 'All right, Emily!' he said. 'We're all done. Could you bring some water for Curly? She's going to be very thirsty.'

Now Jack and Asha were folding up Curly's shorn wool into a bundle. They were giggling. Emily had only come here to be nice to Asha and apologize, but nobody seemed to care. The way the two of them were carrying on, she might not even have existed.

There was a plastic bucket of water by her feet. She picked it up. It was really heavy, and the water slopped from side to side.

The sploshing noise suddenly made Emily remember the swimming pool. Sometimes, when they were waiting for her mum to pick them up, she and her best friend Joanna would sit in the little café area in the leisure centre. They'd have a milkshake and look down on the other kids jumping in and out of the water. She and Joanna used to make bets on who would make the biggest splash. Joanna was probably there right now, sipping milkshake and giggling with Claire. She'd never think about her one-time best friend Emily Keane now.

Emily gripped the handle of the bucket. Her head felt tight and sore. She had no one to laugh and joke with in her new life. She probably never would, either. She'd just go on being lonely and left out for ever.

She felt so miserable that she forgot to watch the bucket. Some of the water slopped over the side and onto the floor. Emily stepped on the wet straw where the water had fallen. Her foot slipped sideways and she lost her balance and fell flat on her face.

The bucket flew up in the air and the water ran out of it like a tidal wave. It went all over Asha.

'Ahhhh!' Asha squealed, leaping to her feet.

Curly gave a loud bleat in panic and twisted her body, trying to escape. In her fear, she bumped against Rory's arm. He lost control of the shears and their sharp points stabbed into the ewe's side.

Emily watched in horror as a red line appeared on Curly's white skin. Slowly the line grew darker, as blood oozed out.

Jack gave a groan. 'Oh, no!'

Asha burst into tears.

Rory shouted for someone to bring a first-aid kit.

Emily sat up in the straw, rubbing her knee where she'd banged it. She'd only been trying to help, but once again everything had gone wrong.

Everyone stopped shouting and turned to look at her.

'I didn't mean to do it!' she yelled, and limped out of the stable as fast as she could.

Chapter Seven

Emily crouched under the chicken shed. She was shivering, and her teeth were chattering, not so much from the cold but from the awfulness of what had just happened.

'I didn't mean it,' she whispered. 'I lost my balance. I couldn't help dropping the bucket.'

Patch was lying next to her. She gave a little whine, as if she understood exactly what Emily was saying.

'Everything goes wrong for me. I was only trying to be nice to Curly and now she's hurt! I try so hard to be good, but it never works.'

Emily's voice felt croaky and sore, but she couldn't stop telling Patch how she felt. The words just kept tumbling out.

'Nobody likes me. Nobody talks to me. They laugh

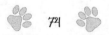

at me, like Jack and Asha just now. They laughed at school when I forgot the words of that poem, at the Easter assembly. They looked at me as if I was weird. Even my dad did…'

A horrible choking feeling rose up in Emily's throat.

'Dad doesn't want me any more, Patch. Denise doesn't want me.'

Patch whined again. She put her paw on Emily's leg.

'They've got Leon now … their baby … he's the only thing they care about…' Hot tears spilled out of Emily's eyes and trickled down her face. It was so hard to speak, but still the words kept coming:

'And they've got each other, Dad and Denise. I haven't got anybody. Nobody knows who I am any more. Mum did … she always knew when I…'

Emily couldn't go on. Her chest hurt with the pain of remembering. Her mum only had to look at her face to know if she was upset about something. She always knew exactly what would make Emily feel better. Sometimes it was a daft joke, to make her laugh. Sometimes it was time to think things through by herself, and then her mum wouldn't say anything, but just bring her a drink and smile at her. And sometimes, the best times, it was a cuddle.

The pain was so strong now that Emily couldn't bear it any more. 'She's gone, Patch – nobody wants me now…' she stammered, and then, even though she knew it wouldn't help, she cried out: '*Mum, come back! Please, come back – I need you!*'

But it was no use. Mum was dead and was never coming back. Emily's body hurt from crying, and her cheeks felt raw where the tracks of her hot, salty tears had run down.

Then something warm brushed against her face.

'Oh!' Emily gasped.

Sometimes, when she was very tiny, her mum used to give her a 'butterfly kiss'. She would flutter her eyelashes against Emily's cheek as if a beautiful butterfly had landed there.

Emily shivered. There it was again. A soft, warm touch against her sore face. She opened her eyes. Patch was licking away the tears from her cheeks.

'Oh, Patch! Thank you.'

Emily put her arms round her. The dog's black and white coat was so soft as she snuggled close.

'We're just the same, aren't we?' Emily whispered. 'Nobody wants us. That's why we've been sent here, because nobody wants us.'

She hugged Patch tightly, and then she bent down

and kissed the tangled fur on top of her head.

'Don't worry, little one,' she said. '*I* want you. No one will find us here. We're safe. I won't let anyone take you away.'

Chapter Eight

'She can't just have disappeared,' Rory said, when Jack and Asha returned to Curly's stable with the news that Emily was nowhere to be found.

'We looked everywhere,' Asha explained. 'I hunted all through the flower garden and the vegetable garden – and I looked in the guinea pigs' shed. Jack searched the horses' stables and Cynthia's sty and the goats' enclosure *and* the cow's field. Kerry did the barn and the café and … and…'

Asha's breath ran out. She felt very hot. She'd been running all over the farm ever since Emily disappeared and now she was completely shattered.

Rory smiled. 'I get the picture. Well done, lass. Top marks for trying.' He got up. 'No need to fret. I might be able to find her. Jack – I need you and Asha to stop here with Curly and keep an eye on her. All right?'

'Sure.' Jack knelt down and gave Curly a gentle pat. 'You'll be fine,' he said to her. 'I've seen five baby lambs born in one night – did you know that?'

The ewe nuzzled his arm. Her golden-brown eyes still had an anxious look in them, but she didn't move when Jack and Asha sat down beside her in the straw.

'Great, there you are!' Kerry ran over to Rory as he stood by the duck pond. 'There's still no sign of her.'

Kerry's face was shiny with sweat, and her braids had bits of leaf caught in them from where she'd looked under the hedge and through the bushes for Emily.

'If she's left the farm, anything could happen to her...' Kerry continued.

'The lass is fine...' Rory tried to reassure her.

'But she's just vanished into thin air!'

Rory held a finger to his lips. Kerry looked at him, puzzled, as he gestured for her to tiptoe after him towards the chicken shed. When they got there, he knelt down on the ground.

Kerry knelt down too, straining her eyes to see into the grotty, gloomy space under the shed. She could just make out the shape of a girl, crouching down, stroking a small dog.

'It's Emily!' Kerry cried. 'You found her!'

Emily's heart leaped as if it would jump right out of her body when she heard Kerry's voice. She turned cold with misery. She'd promised Patch they'd be safe here. There was no escape now. They were trapped under the shed, with no way out.

The dog sensed Emily's fear and struggled to get out of her arms.

Rory was there too. Emily could see the white tufts of his hair as he bent down to peer at them. Her heart thudded against her chest. He was going to come under and pull them out!

'Leave us alone!' she cried, and Patch, really panicking now, freed herself from Emily's hug and fled to her corner.

'It's all right, lass. Don't worry,' Rory said gently.

Emily shivered as she remembered those accusing eyes, staring at her in Curly's stable.

'Go away!' she cried.

'We're so glad we've found you' Kerry said. 'We know you didn't mean for Curly to get hurt.'

Emily didn't believe her. 'I'm not coming out!' she shouted.

'Hey − that's Patch hiding in the corner, isn't it?'

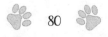

80

Rory asked.

'You're frightening her. Go away!'

Rory stayed where he was. 'You've been taking care of her. Well done, Emily.'

'She's scared. Can't you just leave us alone?'

'She's not scared of you, lass. You've got a way with animals,' Rory said.

'No I haven't! Look at what I did to Curly.'

Rory looked puzzled. 'That wasn't your fault. If you're looking for someone to blame, then it should be me. I was the one holding the shears. I should have taken more care—'

'Shh!' Kerry interrupted. 'We saw you fall, Emily. It was an accident. You didn't mean to throw the water. Curly panicked, and bumped into the shears. It wasn't your fault.'

Emily felt tears start to well in her eyes. 'It's always my fault when something goes wrong!'

Kerry sighed. 'That's the last time I want to hear you say that, Emily Keane, because it's rubbish. Curly will be fine. The cut was just a scratch.'

Emily's head swam with confusion. Kerry was cross, but not about Curly. She was angry with Emily for blaming herself for the accident. Maybe it wasn't her fault, after all.

'Emily, Patch needs help,' Rory said. 'We have to get her cleaned up and into the warm. You're the only person who can persuade her to come out. Can you do it?'

Emily reached her hand out to Patch. 'It's OK,' she whispered. 'They won't hurt you.'

Patch gave a little whine and wriggled towards her, keeping her belly flat to the ground.

Very slowly, Emily crawled out from under the shed, and Patch, shivering nervously, followed her. Then she lay on Emily's feet, pressed right up against her legs, and looked up at her with anxious eyes.

Rory beamed. 'Don't tell me you haven't got a way with animals!' he said, his voice warm and proud. 'You're a natural, lass.'

'Emily – you're a star!' Kerry added.

Emily's heart swelled with pride. She bent down to stroke Patch's head.

Kerry said, 'Look at those knots in her coat. She really needs a bath.'

Rory nodded. 'Take her up to the farmhouse. You can use my bathroom, and no one will disturb you. Emily, you're the only human Patch trusts right now, so you're in charge.'

Emily's heart turned over. Rory seemed to

understand about her and Patch. But how could he know how the two of them had got together and become so close? She'd been so careful to keep it a secret.

'Come on, Emily,' Kerry said. 'I'll let you in to the farmhouse. Rory needs to get back and see how Curly's doing.'

Emily looked at Rory anxiously. 'Curly will be OK, won't she?'

Rory nodded and smiled. 'Aye, she'll be grand.'

Kerry put her arm round Emily's shoulders and steered her up the path. Patch followed behind, her nose close to Emily's heels.

Rory's bathroom was a good place to bathe a dog, Emily thought, as she turned on the hot and cold taps. It was right up under the roof of the old farmhouse, with wooden beams in the sloping ceiling. And there weren't masses of bottles and jars and hairclips and baby things scattered everywhere, like there were at home. Just a razor, a comb and a toothbrush on the shelf by the sink and a white bar of soap on the side of the bath.

Kerry was spreading some towels on the floor. 'Good girl, Patch,' she said, as Emily lifted the dog over the side of the bath and laid her in the warm water. 'She trusts you so much, Emily. Here, use this.' She gave Emily a bottle of dog shampoo.

'I understand her,' Emily said, squeezing some shampoo onto her hands and rubbing it gently into Patch's coat. 'We're both the same. Nobody wants us.'

'That's not true—' Kerry started to say.

'It is,' Emily interrupted. 'Jack and Asha were really annoyed when I spilled that water. They must think I'm useless.'

Kerry shook her head. 'They came with me to look for you. They were really worried.'

Emily shrugged. 'But they're not my friends. I haven't got any friends now.'

Kerry smiled. 'I know how that feels!'

Emily stared at her. Kerry was so pretty, with her lovely smile, her warm brown eyes and her wonderful braids with their silver beads. She was dead cool.

'How come? I bet everyone wants to be your friend.'

Kerry looked sad. 'When I was fifteen, my dad got a new job and we had to move to this city. I left behind my best friend, my schoolmates – and my grown-up sister and her baby. Just about everyone I was close to.' She shook out her long black braids, as if she was banishing the painful memory. 'I was so lonely.

Everyone at my new school had their own friends. Nobody cared about me.'

'That's awful,' Emily said, stroking shampoo over Patch's head, taking care not to get any in the dog's eyes.

'I still had Mum though, to go home to.'

Emily kept her eyes on the soapy water in the bath. She didn't want to cry in front of Kerry. It hurt to think now nice it would be if her mum was still alive and waiting for her at home. She could bear anything then. She wouldn't care if no one wanted to be friends with her.

'It's been really, really tough for you, Emily, to lose your mum. Anyone would have a hard time fitting in at a new school after what you've been through.'

Emily's throat felt tight. She had to find out though what had happened to Kerry.

'Did you make some new friends in the end?' she managed to ask after a moment.

Kerry nodded and started to smile. 'It took a while though. I couldn't believe that anyone could be as close to me as Jenny, my old best friend. But then I got to know some of my new classmates, and I really liked them. I still see one or two of them even now.'

'I don't think it'll ever be like that for me,' Emily

said, remembering all the staring faces in the assembly hall. And the way that Jack and Asha would rather laugh and giggle with each other than talk to her.

'When bad things happen, Emily, it can take a long time for us to trust people again. Just look at Patch!'

Kerry reached her hand out and Patch shivered and backed away, splashing through the bath water.

Emily rubbed her ears and told her in a gentle voice not to be silly. Patch stopped shivering and licked her hand. She looked up at Emily and her eyes shone with happiness.

'See?' Kerry said. 'She trusts you. In spite of all the bad things that have happened to her, she wants to be your friend.'

Emily stroked Patch's head. Kerry was right. If Patch, who'd been treated so cruelly by humans, could learn to trust again, maybe she could too. Things would never be the same as they were when her mum was still alive, but maybe there was a chance she could be happy again.

Chapter Nine

Emily couldn't wait to tell her dad what Rory'd said to her. *You've got a way with animals. You're a natural, lass!* He'd be so proud of her, when he knew she'd won Patch's trust – something that nobody else on the farm could do.

But Dad wasn't there when she got home. He was still at work and Denise said that he'd be late back. She'd made a shepherd's pie, with a crispy cheese-and-potato topping, for their supper. It was lot nicer than the ready-meals that she warmed up in the microwave when she was too tired and too busy with Leon to cook.

Emily ate up everything on her plate. She was hungry after all the excitement of her day at the farm. After she'd helped Denise to load up the dishwasher, she went through to the living room and lay on the sofa. She couldn't stop thinking about Patch. How was she feeling now, all on her own again?

The little dog had been upset, whining and trembling when Emily had to leave. She wouldn't stay with Rory at the farmhouse. She didn't want to follow Kerry into the barn, either. The only person she wanted to be with was Emily.

Rory had been very patient. He'd told Emily not to worry. If Patch wasn't confident enough yet to be with other people and come indoors, he would set up a proper dog bed for her in her favourite corner under the chicken shed. She'd feel safe there overnight, and she'd be really pleased to see Emily again in the morning. Over the next few days, Rory explained, they could work on building up her confidence. There was no need to rush.

It gave Emily a warm feeling inside, to think that she'd be with Patch again tomorrow, as soon as she got back to the farm.

Denise came through into the living room. Her face looked blotchy and her hair was all messy where she'd tried to pin it up and Leon had pulled it down again.

'Emily, would you be a love and sit with Leon for half an hour? He's just dropped off, and I really need to have a bath and wash my hair.'

Emily said she didn't mind. If her baby brother was asleep, she could stay on the sofa and read.

'Great.' Denise brought Leon's carry-chair through. He was lying in it with his eyes closed and his little arms stretched out. Denise put the chair on the floor next to Emily and went upstairs to run her bath.

Emily rummaged in her bag, searching for one of her favourite books. Instead, she found the diary that Kerry had given her. Emily thought back over today, and suddenly she didn't want to read. She had a story to tell now – the story of how she and Patch became friends. She opened the diary at the first blank page, found a felt-tip and wrote: *Patch and Me.*

From upstairs there was a noise of water running, and Denise's footsteps padding along the landing. She must be just getting into her bath.

'Great!' Emily sighed. Hopefully Denise would be lolling around in the hot water for ages.

How should she begin writing the story? Some people started off with '*Dear Diary*'. But a diary wasn't a person. This one was just an empty exercise book. She could write the story for her dad, but it would be a lot more fun to tell him out loud. Emily's heart jumped as she thought of someone else she could write it for. Her mum! More than anyone else in the world, her mum would have understood how much Emily loved Patch.

Dear Mum, she began, *I know you will never read this, but I want to write and tell you anyway. Something really good happened. I made a new friend. She's a dog, called Patch. I know you'd like her...*

Denise was making sloshing noises upstairs in the bath, but Emily didn't notice. Her felt-tip raced across the page, as in her mind she was back at the farm, coaxing Patch out from under the chicken shed, and hearing Rory say: *You're a natural.*

She wrote on and on, until she'd covered three whole pages. She put the last full stop in place and closed the diary. Then she felt empty and sad. It was fun writing about Patch, but her mum would never read it. And when her dad came home, he probably wouldn't care, either. He wouldn't have time to listen to her. He'd go straight to Leon and start making a fuss of him.

She sighed and looked down at Leon in his chair. He was still fast asleep. His hair was sticking up in a curl on top of his head and his eyelashes looked very long where they lay on his round cheeks. Now that he wasn't yelling and shouting and making a mess everywhere, he actually looked quite cute.

As Emily watched him, he made a snuffling noise and his small hands twitched. She got off the sofa and knelt down beside him, worried in case he was going to wake up, but he was just dreaming. He looked so peaceful, snuggled up in his chair. He was just a baby, small and helpless. It wasn't his fault he'd made her life so miserable.

She reached out and touched his face with the tip of her finger. His cheek felt so soft. Emily just had to stroke it.

'You're a cutie,' she whispered.

Leon wriggled. He opened his eyes and blinked at her. 'Mmmm!' he said, and smiled at her; a big, toothless grin.

'Hi!' Emily said, and grinned back.

Leon said 'Mmmm!' again. Then he turned his head and looked round the living room as if he was searching for Denise. When he couldn't see her, he stopped smiling. His round face crumpled into a frown.

'Don't, Leon, please!' Emily begged.

It was no good. Her baby brother took a deep breath. His face, that looked so sweet just a moment before, turned bright red. He opened his mouth and began to scream.

'*Waaah! Waaah!*'

Leon's yells were so loud that Emily's ears were ringing. She tried to calm him down by rocking his chair, but he just screamed even more.

'What are you *doing* to him?' Denise rushed into the living room in her dressing gown, a towel wrapped round her head.

'Nothing … I…' Emily was about to explain that he'd just woken up and started yelling when she heard the sound of a key in the front door. Her dad was home.

He came into the living room and threw his briefcase down on an armchair. 'What's all this?' he asked.

'There, there, sweetheart.' Denise held Leon against her shoulder and patted his back. 'I asked Emily to look after him for five minutes and look what's happened. Honestly, Jonathan, I'm at the end of my tether.'

'I didn't do anything!' Emily shouted, trying to make herself heard over Leon's roars.

'Emily, go to your room!' her dad snapped.

'You're always telling me to go to my room,' she shouted back. 'It's not fair!'

Her dad looked down at her. He looked really tired and really fed-up.

'I didn't mean to upset him,' Emily said. 'I was just—'

'Emily, do as you're told,' Dad interrupted. 'Go to your room!' He went over to Denise and put his arms around her and Leon.

Emily picked up her things – her bag, the diary and the felt-tip. 'All right, I will!' she said.

No one took any notice of her. Leon was howling louder than ever. Denise was crying too. She leaned her head on Dad's shoulder and he put his arms round her. They didn't even look round as Emily ran out of the living room.

Outside Emily's bedroom window, the moon was shining and little silver clouds were racing across the night sky.

It was very windy. She remembered what Kerry had said about the weather forecast, when they were picking the daffodils. It didn't matter though, even if a gale was blowing. However bad the weather was, nothing was going to stop her now. Emily was leaving home tonight, and she would never come back.

The house was quiet. Her dad and Denise had come

upstairs to bed. Emily had heard their feet thumping on the landing as they carried Leon into his room. Then she'd heard them muttering to each other. She couldn't make out what they were saying, but they must have been talking about her. Saying what a nuisance she was. Dad had knocked on her door but she'd ignored him and pretended to be asleep. What was the point in answering him if she was only going to get told off again?

I won't be for much longer, Emily thought.

She rolled up a spare pair of jeans and a couple of tops and stuffed them into her bag, along with a change of socks and underwear. They wouldn't miss her, when she was gone. They'd be much happier without her. A proper little family. Dad, Mum and baby.

No one would care that Emily wasn't around any more, making trouble and messing things up. A tear slid down her face as she thought of how sweet Leon had looked, fast asleep in his chair. Why did he have to start crying, the moment he saw her?

Emily looked round at her bedroom, silently saying 'goodbye' to all her things. On the dressing table there was a photo of her mum, smiling and happy, the way she was before she got ill and had to go into hospital.

Emily had taken the picture, one day when they had gone to the park.

There was just enough room in the bag for the photo in its frame. Emily picked it up and stuffed it inside, before pulling the zip closed. Then she tiptoed downstairs, opened the front door and stepped out into the cold moonlight.

'I'm coming to get you, Patch,' she whispered, though no one could hear but the silent moon and the clouds that flew past above her head. 'We'll go somewhere far away, you and me, where no one will ever be horrible to us again.'

Chapter Ten

The City Farm gate cast a spooky black shadow in the moonlight. Emily had never been outside so late at night before. Her skin prickled as she heard a rustling noise behind her.

She turned round, holding her breath in fear, but it was just a crisps packet blowing along the pavement in the wind. That's all it was, just a piece of litter.

Her hands were freezing cold after the long walk. She pushed the gate. It didn't open. She grabbed the bars and shook them, but nothing happened. Rory must have locked up before he went off to bed at the farmhouse.

Emily didn't know what to do. She looked all around. No one was about. The grass in the park shone silver under the moon, and the streets that led into the council estate were empty, except for a few parked cars. There was no one she could ask for help.

On the other side of the flats, a police siren wailed. Emily's heart raced. Maybe it was looking for her! Perhaps her dad had rung the police station to report her as a missing person. Maybe he'd looked in her bedroom and seen her empty bed. If only she'd thought to put a bundle of clothes under the covers, to make it look like she was still there...

The noise of the siren was getting closer. Emily ducked into the shadows and ran alongside the tall wooden fence that surrounded the farm. She kept going until she found herself in a dark alleyway, where the bins that belonged to the flats were kept. There were plenty of hiding places here.

A four-legged shape stepped out from among the bins.

'Patch?' Emily gasped, her heart thudding.

But this creature wasn't Patch. Its legs were too thin and it had a sharp, pointed nose. It came closer to Emily, sniffing the air to catch her smell. She held her breath, and saw its red-brown coat glinting in the moonlight. It was a fox.

She kept very still and watched as the fox trotted off and rummaged along the bottom of the fence.

Suddenly it disappeared. There must be a gap in the planks!

Emily ran over. Sure enough, there was a place where one of the planks had been broken. She knelt down and peered through the hole. All she could see of the farm were grass and twigs.

'Patch!' she called softly, not daring to shout in case someone in the flats heard her. 'Are you there?'

She whistled and called again, but there was no sign of the little dog. Patch must be fast asleep under the chicken shed. There was nothing for it. Emily had to get into the farm and fetch her. But she was much bigger than the skinny fox. How was she going to squeeze through the gap?

She pushed her bag through and tried to climb after it, but her shoulders were too wide and she stuck fast between the planks.

Don't panic! she told herself, as her head swam with fear. She took a deep breath and willed herself not to cry. *There must be a way to get through.* She wriggled around until she was on her side. Then she pushed and struggled to force herself through the gap.

It was a very tight squeeze, but somehow Emily made it. She fell onto the wet grass on her hands and knees. She was in the garden area, where the runner beans and other vegetables grew.

'Thank you!' she whispered to the dark hedgerow where the fox must be hiding.

Suddenly a tall figure with ragged sleeves that fluttered in the wind and a huge, floppy hat on its head loomed towards her, stretching out its long arms.

Emily screamed. It was the figure from her nightmares, the gruesome monster that had stolen her mum. And now it was coming after her!

She closed her eyes, expecting to feel the monster's rough hands grabbing hold of her hair. Her heart was kicking inside her like a trapped rabbit. Nothing happened. After a moment she opened her eyes. The tattered, scary figure was still in the same place.

Emily gasped with relief. It was only Rory the Second. The wind had got inside the scarecrow's coat, making it look as if it was alive. She hugged her bag to her chest and hurried on.

As she passed Curly's stable, a faint light shone out over the door. Someone must be inside! Emily slowed down, tiptoeing past. Then she heard something that made her whole body turn icy cold.

'*Urgh!*' A weird noise, like a groan or a cough.

Emily froze to the spot. What was happening in the stable?

'*Urgh! Uurrgh!*' Whoever was making the noise sounded as if they were in pain.

'Hello?' Emily called. No one answered. The groan came again.

A terrible thought came into Emily's mind. What if it was Curly who was crying out like this?

She crept up to the stable door. Curly was stretched out on a mound of straw. Somebody had left a lantern hanging in the corner of the stable, which shone a pool of yellow light over her white body.

'What's the matter, Curly?'

The ewe lifted her head and looked at Emily with wide, frightened eyes. The cut on her side wasn't bleeding. It seemed to be fine.

Suddenly Curly's body twisted with pain. It was almost as if she was fighting against something inside herself that was hurting her.

'*Uurrgh!*' she groaned. She looked round at her side and then her head fell back onto the straw and she made a little choking noise.

Now Emily understood what was happening. 'Curly – it's your lamb!' she cried. 'It's being born! Wait there – I'll get help!'

Emily completely forgot that she'd come to the farm to find Patch and run away with her. She dropped her bag and raced up the path to the farmhouse. All the windows were dark and there was no doorbell on the old wooden door. Emily banged and banged on it with her fists and yelled as loud as she could:

'Please, come quick! It's Curly!'

Her hands were sore from thumping on the hard wood before a light flicked on upstairs.

It took ages for Rory to come to the door. She was just going to start thumping again, to make him hurry up, when there was a *tick-tick* sound of claws trotting over the concrete behind her. Next thing, a cold nose nudged her hand. As Emily turned round, Patch leaped in the air and licked her hand.

'Patch!' Emily threw her arms around the little dog.

Patch's tail was wagging wildly, and she jumped up again and again to greet Emily, as if she was trying to tell her how happy she was to see her.

The front door creaked open and Rory looked out, his white hair sticking up like tufts of Curly's fleece. He blinked sleepily. 'What's going on?'

'It's the lamb! Curly's having her baby!'

'Right.' Rory shook himself awake. He grabbed a coat from the hook on the wall and put it on over his pyjamas. Then he shoved his bare feet into a large pair of wellingtons. 'Let's go!' He stopped and looked down at Emily. 'Whatever are you doing here? It's the middle of the night!'

'Please, there's no time! Curly needs us!'

Rory nodded. 'Right.'

The two of them ran along the path together, Patch racing close behind.

As soon as Rory heard Curly's groans, his face turned very serious. He went straight into the stable and knelt down beside her.

'You're having a bad time, poor lass.' He turned to Emily. 'Come here and sit by her head.' He spoke quickly, in a brisk tone she'd never heard him use before. 'Give her a scratch. Try and soothe her. I'm going to deliver the lamb.'

Rory went to crouch down by Curly's tail and Emily stroked the ewe under her velvety chin.

'We're here now, Curly, it's all right,' she whispered. Patch came and sat down on the floor next to her.

The ewe thrashed around as wave after wave of pain gripped her body. Her eyes were dull and her tongue was hanging out of the side of her mouth as she groaned and grunted.

Emily kept on telling her everything would be all right.

'Poor lass, she's been struggling away on her own

for a long time,' Rory said. 'Keep going, Curly! Not long now.'

Curly gave one last groan. Her whole body shuddered and then she lay flat, gasping for breath on the straw.

'Brave lass, well done!' Rory said in a gentle voice. He looked up at Emily and told her to come and see.

Emily hurried to join him. There, curled up on the straw, was a very small baby lamb. Its woolly coat was wet and sticky and it was lying very still.

'Is it alive?' Emily whispered.

'I think so. We just need to get her breathing.'

Rory got a cloth and rubbed the lamb's head and sides until she coughed and spluttered. The tiny creature stared up at Emily with big dark eyes. Then she opened its mouth, and gave a wobbly 'Baaa!'

'Hey, Curly – listen!' Rory said with a huge smile. 'That's your little daughter!'

Chapter Eleven

'She's amazing!' Emily breathed, gazing down at the new arrival.

The baby ewe was perfect, with her tiny cloven hoofs and her short, tightly curled coat.

Rory was busy looking after Curly. He brought her some water, but she didn't drink it. He picked up her baby and held it close to her nose, but the ewe just closed her eyes and ignored the lamb.

He frowned. 'Summat's not right here.'

Emily's stomach dropped. Curly was so still, stretched out on the straw. 'What's wrong? She's not going to die, is she?'

'She's in a bad way. I have to call the vet.'

Rory carried the lamb to the side of the stable where there was a big pile of clean straw.

'Come and give her a cuddle. Keep her safe while I'm gone.'

Emily sat on the straw and hugged the lamb's little body. The tiny ewe was very warm from having been inside her mother, and her small heart was beating fast. Patch came and lay down beside Emily and licked her hand.

'I'm glad you're here, Patch,' she said softly. She felt very afraid as she looked over at Curly. The ewe was still breathing; Emily could see her side moving slowly up and down. But there was no other sign of life at all. The vet had better come soon.

It wasn't long before Emily heard the sound of Rory's footsteps hurrying up the path.

'Vet's on his way,' he said, coming into the stable. 'Now, we need to get that little one to have a drink.' He knelt down beside Curly and pulled a small bowl out of his pocket. 'I'm going to milk her,' he said. 'A new-born lamb needs the colostrum from its mother right away.'

'What's that?' Emily asked. She'd never heard of 'colostrum' before.

'It's the first milk the ewe makes. It's very special – full of antibodies and vitamins and all sorts of good things to get the baby lamb off to a good start.'

Rory squeezed Curly's udder, milking her into the bowl. Then he showed the bowl to Emily. It was full of a thick yellow liquid.

'Yuck! That looks horrible!'

Rory grinned. 'Believe me, it's the best thing in the world for that little creature right now.' He rummaged in his other pocket and pulled out a bottle. He filled it with the yellowy milk and fitted a teat on top of it. 'Watch carefully, Emily.' He lifted the lamb onto her feet and then he knelt down, holding her between his knees with her small nose facing away from him. 'This is how we feed a new-born lamb.'

'Shouldn't you cuddle her?' Emily asked. 'She looks too weak to stand up.'

Rory shook his head. 'This is how she would feed from her mum,' he said. 'She needs to be on her feet, or she won't be able to digest properly.'

He held the bottle in front of the lamb's face. But the tiny animal didn't want the milk. She just stood there with her head drooping.

Rory looked worried. 'We need to get this little one into the barn where it's warm. But I can't leave Curly till the vet gets here.'

'I could take her,' Emily said, but she felt really scared. What if she couldn't get the lamb to feed? It was such a big responsibility. Even Rory couldn't do it.

'That would be great,' Rory said. 'I'll be up there as soon as the vet arrives.' He picked up the lamb and gave her to Emily. 'If anyone can do it, you can,' he said.

It felt odd to be inside the barn at night. It was so quiet and empty. No Kerry, talking on the phone. No clinking of plates and smells of food from the café. No Jack and no Asha, chatting and laughing together.

There was still a glow of red from the logs in the stove. Emily got a cushion from the sofa and put it on the floor, right in front of the stove. She knelt on the cushion, holding the lamb between her knees just as Rory had shown her. Patch lay on the floor beside them, watching Emily's every move.

The baby lamb was just the same as she'd been a few moments ago, with Rory. She didn't want to suck from the bottle. Every time Emily tried to feed her, she turned her head away.

'Come on, little one,' Emily said. 'Please try.' Her voice sounded weird and echoey in the empty barn.

She wiggled the teat of the bottle against the lamb's lips, remembering what Denise did when Leon didn't want his milk. But it was no use. The lamb wouldn't suck.

'Please!' Emily whispered. The tiny creature was so weak and skinny. What if she was ill? If she didn't have the special milk soon, she might not survive. A hot tear welled up in Emily's eye and slid down her cheek. She bit her lip to stop it trembling. Patch whined, and nudged Emily with her nose.

'What's up, Patch?'

The dog stood up, her tail wagging, and sniffed at the baby ewe. Then she licked the little animal's neck and her woolly shoulder.

The lamb wriggled and gave a bleat. She lifted up her head and looked around, as if she was searching for something. Patch kept on licking.

Emily tried with the bottle again, and this time the lamb seized hold of it in her mouth and started sucking.

'Oh, Patch – well done!' Emily gasped.

The lamb sucked and sucked until the milk was all gone. When the bottle was empty, she looked around the barn again, and gave a loud 'Baaa!'

'I bet she's looking for her mum,' Emily said. Patch wagged her tail, looking up at Emily with bright eyes. 'I know!' Emily had an idea. She got up from the cushion and laid the lamb down on it. Then she patted the cushion. 'Patch, up!'

Patch understood what Emily meant right away. She climbed up on the cushion and lay down next to the baby ewe so that they were curled up together. At once the lamb closed her eyes and snuggled close to the dog.

Emily stroked Patch's head. 'Clever girl!'

The two animals looked so peaceful, so close and warm, lying there on the cushion. When Emily's mum was still alive they used to lie on the sofa together in the evening after supper. Her mum would wrap her arms round Emily and they'd cuddle up, and sometimes they'd read or watch the television, and sometimes they'd just lie there and talk.

She stroked the lamb's head. The little creature blinked at her.

'I've thought of a name for you,' she said. 'It's Lizzie. That was my mum's name. Would you like that?'

Lizzie nodded her head. Emily smiled, but then she realized that the lamb was just nodding with tiredness.

'All right, Lizzie,' she said. 'Go to sleep. Patch will take care of you. Patch will be your mum for now.'

Her heart suddenly shrank inside her. Lizzie didn't

need her now. Patch didn't need her. They had each other. Without the little dog beside her, Emily felt empty and alone. The cold, painful feeling that swelled up in her chest hurt so much she could hardly bear it.

She crept over to the sofa and lay down with her arms wrapped round herself. What was it Kerry had said to her? *Sometimes feelings are so strong they just take you over.* It was like that now. Sadness and loneliness were freezing her up, turning her body into a lump of ice.

But Kerry had told her to write about her feelings. She'd said it would help. Emily's bag was next to her on the sofa. Her head felt heavy and her arms ached, but she reached for the bag and pulled out the diary.

She opened it, and saw all the words she'd written about Patch, earlier that night. All the happy stuff. She turned to the next clean page.

Dear Mum, she wrote. *Why did you have to leave me? I miss you. I wish you would just walk through the door right now and come and sit with me on the sofa and give me a cuddle. Nobody hugs me now. Nobody talks to me. Nobody cares what happens to me. I tried to be nice to Leon, but I just made him cry. He hates me so much he screams every time he sees me. Dad hates me. Denise hates me. They don't want me. I came to the farm tonight to get Patch so we could go away somewhere, just the two of us...*

Big, hot tears ran down Emily's face. She was shaking so much she could hardly hold the felt-tip, but she managed to scrawl down a few final words, in big untidy letters that took up nearly a whole page.

MUM! PLEASE, PLEASE COME BACK! I NEED YOU...

Emily didn't hear the creak of the barn door opening, or the sound of footsteps running towards her. She didn't realize she was no longer alone until a voice said:

'Emily! What's going on?'

It was her dad.

Chapter Twelve

'Dad! What are you doing here?' Emily gasped.

'We got a phone call,' Dad said. His glasses were lopsided and his hair was sticking up. He looked as if he'd just jumped out of bed, thrown his coat on and driven straight to the farm. 'Rory … called us. He said you were here. I've been going crazy with worry.'

Emily waited for her dad to tell her off. But he didn't.

He just ran his fingers through his hair and said: 'It's the middle of the night, Em. We were all fast asleep. I don't understand – you've been at the farm all day, why did you want to come back now?'

Emily's stomach flipped over, and her face went very hot. Her dad didn't realize that she'd meant to run away. He thought she'd just crept out of the house and come to visit the farm. Then he looked down and saw Emily's bag, with the zip wide open. He gave a little gasp of shock when he saw the spare clothes and the photo of her mum.

'Oh, Em!'

Emily couldn't look at him. Now he knew what she'd been planning to do, he'd be really angry with her.

All he said was, 'You were running away. But why, love?'

She swallowed. It was hard to say the words, but she made herself do it.

'I thought you'd be happy, you and Denise, without me. All I do is cause trouble. I just get in the way and make Leon cry.'

Her dad blinked, staring at her as if he was trying to understand what she'd just said.

'I thought it would be better if I left.'

'Em, *no!*' Her dad sat down on the sofa next to her. 'You've got it all wrong.'

'But you're always angry with me.'

'Sweetheart, I may be cross sometimes, but it's not because of you. I'm just so tired, that's all. With work and with the baby. It's the same for Denise. She's exhausted. We both are, all the time.' He sighed and rubbed his face with the back of his hand. Then he reached out and put his arm round Emily's shoulders. 'You're our best girl, Em. We love you.'

'But you love Leon more,' Emily said. 'You don't really want me around.'

Her dad pulled her close to him. 'That's crazy. We love you very much, we all do.'

He looked down and saw the diary lying open on the floor.

'No, that's private…' Emily began, but she was too late. He'd already picked it up and opened it. 'Please, Dad – don't look at it!'

Emily grabbed the diary from him. She wriggled along the sofa, so he couldn't get it back.

'What were you writing about, love?'

'Nothing!' Emily shook her head.

'I'd love to read it.'

'No!' Emily clutched the diary to her chest.

'It might help me to understand how you feel. Please, Em.'

Emily looked at her dad and was shocked to see that his eyes were full of tears. She opened the diary and looked at the first page. At the words she'd written in the living room, when Leon was asleep in his chair. She'd wanted so badly to tell her dad about Patch.

Maybe she could do that now.

'I'll read you the first bit, if you like,' she said.

'That would be great,' Dad said softly.

'*Dear Mum,*' she began, reading aloud from the beginning of the diary. '*I know you will never read this, but I want to write and tell you anyway. Something really good happened. I made a new friend. She's a dog, called Patch—*'

'But why didn't you tell *me* about this?' her dad interrupted.

'I tried to. But Leon was crying, and Denise wanted you.'

'Oh, Em. I'm so sorry. Please read some more.'

'*Patch is just like me. Nobody wants her. Nobody cares about her. She's afraid of all human beings except me. I gave her a bath today, and she wouldn't let anybody else do that. The first time we met, she just ran away, but then I found her again...*'

Dad sat and listened while Emily read to him. He didn't say anything, just looked down at his hands. When she finished the part where Rory said she was a 'natural' with animals, Emily closed the diary and put it down.

Dad put his arms round her and gave her a very big hug. Emily could feel that his face was wet with tears.

'I'm so sorry,' he said over and over again. 'Is that Patch over there, lying in front of the fire?'

Emily nodded, her face pressed tightly against Dad's jacket.

'And who's that?' Dad gently let go of her and leaned forward, peering at the cushion.

'She's Lizzie, the baby lamb,' Emily explained. She told her dad how she'd found Curly just about to give birth. 'Curly's very poorly now. Rory had to send for the vet. Lizzie misses her mum. That's why she's with Patch.'

'Lizzie?' Dad said.

Emily looked down at the floor and nodded.

'You miss your mum a lot, don't you, Em?' Dad said softly.

'All the time,' Emily said. She felt his arm going around her shoulders.

'Did you write about her in the diary too?'

Emily nodded. 'But I don't want to read it out, Dad.'

'Can I read it?'

Emily didn't want him to. But he was being so kind. She felt mean not letting him. She handed him the diary, and curled up beside him, tucking her feet up on the sofa.

Her heart pounded as Dad read the words that she'd written just before he'd arrived, when she'd been feeling so upset. When she'd begged her mum to come back.

Dad closed the diary and sighed. 'I'd give anything for you to have your mum back again,' he said, hugging her to him.

'Really?' Emily looked up at him. Once again his eyes were glassy with tears.

'Of course,' Dad said. He stroked Emily's hair. 'I can't imagine how hard it must have been for you.'

'Kerry said if I wrote down how I felt, it wouldn't hurt so much.'

'Did it work?'

'Maybe. I don't know.' Emily still felt cold inside. Her head throbbed and her chest felt heavy.

Dad put the diary back in Emily's bag. Then he reached out for her hand and squeezed it.

'I'm so sorry I haven't been here for you as much as I should have.'

Emily couldn't answer him, but it was good to feel his warm hand holding hers.

'I love you very much, Em. Denise does too. She thinks the world of you,' he said.

'Does she?' Emily asked.

Dad nodded. 'Of course. She thinks you're clever and funny and pretty. It's just that she's too tired and flustered at the moment to remember to tell you. And Leon adores you. Haven't you ever noticed how his face lights up whenever he sees you?'

Emily remembered back to the moment in the living room, when Leon had woken up and smiled at her.

'But why does he have to cry so much?'

Dad smiled. 'He's a baby. He doesn't know the words to tell us how he feels, so he just has to cry. Believe me, you were just the same!' Dad turned so that he was looking straight at Emily. 'We want you to be happy, Em. We know it's hard for you to have a new brother so soon after losing your mum. And I know Denise and I aren't perfect, but we're your family, and we love you very much.'

Emily nodded.

'No one can step into your mum's shoes,' her dad added, after a moment. 'And you'll always miss her, of course you will. I miss her too. But don't forget that we love you, and together we can get through this.'

Emily looked across to the cushion in front of the fire. Patch had curled herself right around Lizzie, keeping her safe and warm. The dog lifted her head, as if she sensed that Emily was watching her, and she gave a wag of her tail, very gently, so as not to wake her little friend.

Dad's mobile suddenly rang. It sounded very loud in the quiet barn. He stood up to answer it. Patch lifted her head and gave a nervous little bark.

'It's OK, Patch,' Emily reassured her. 'It's only my dad. No need to be scared.'

'Hi, Denise!' Dad said into the phone. 'She's fine, thank goodness. I'm with her now.' He smiled at Emily, then carried on talking: 'We're going to stay here. I'll explain in the morning. Emily needs to be at the farm and I should be with her. All right? Yes – I'll tell her. Love you too!'

He pressed a button on the phone to end the call and put it back in his jacket pocket.

'Denise sends you her love,' he said, sitting down on the sofa once more. 'She's really pleased you're OK.'

He put his arm around her. Emily snuggled up against him. Her dad felt warm and strong as he hugged her. It wasn't quite the same as it used to be, when she lay on the sofa with her mum, but it was lovely to be cuddled again.

'I'm glad you're here, Dad,' she said.

Chapter Thirteen

The City Farm cockerel was crowing, telling everyone it was time to get up. 'Cock-a-doodle-doo!' he called, over and over again.

Emily stretched and yawned. She opened her eyes and saw the big wooden beams of the barn roof high above her. Last night, she and her dad had taken some of the square cushions off the sofa seat and spread them out on the floor. The two of them had lain down side by side on the cushions and fallen asleep straightaway.

Now it was the next day. The stove had gone out and the grey light that came in through the windows promised that it would be damp and misty outside.

'Cock-a-doodle-doo!'

Emily's dad must have heard the cockerel too. He

rolled over on the cushions.

'Em? Are you awake?'

'Yes, Dad.' Emily sat up and yawned again.

Patch and Lizzie were still fast asleep in front of the stove, curled tightly together in a ball.

The door to the barn rattled, and Rory came in, blowing on his cold hands to warm them up. 'Aha, you're awake,' he said. 'When I came by after the vet had gone you were both so sound asleep it seemed a shame to wake you.'

'Is Curly all right?' Emily jumped to her feet. 'What did the vet say?'

'With rest and care she'll be fine. Thanks to you, Miss Keane.'

'Thanks to *me*? I didn't do anything.'

'You knew she was in trouble and you came straight to find me. It would've been a very different outcome if you hadn't. How's the little 'un?'

Emily pointed to where Lizzie and Patch lay on their cushion.

Rory's red face broke into a wide smile. 'Well I never! Great idea, Emily.'

'I've heard of dogs looking after orphaned lambs, but I've never actually seen it before,' Emily's dad said, sitting up and rubbing his eyes. 'It's incredible.'

'Certainly is. Well done, Emily, for thinking of it.'

'It was Patch's idea just as much as mine,' Emily said.

The dog lifted her head at the sound of her name and wagged her tail.

Rory held out his hand to her. 'That's right, lass, we're talking about you.'

This time, Patch didn't back away from him. She even let him stroke her head.

'A lucky day for you, lass, when Emily heard you whining under the chicken shed!' Rory continued.

'I thought that was our secret...' Emily stammered. How did Rory find out?

Rory smiled. 'After we fed the chickens the other day, I saw you creeping under the shed. I heard you talking to her. So I left you both alone to get acquainted.'

Emily didn't know whether to feel pleased or shy as she learned that Rory had known all along about her and Patch becoming friends.

'I heard all about this last night. Amazing!' Mr Keane said.

Rory chuckled. 'She's got a wonderful way with animals, your lass. We'll make a farmer of her yet.'

A thrill of excitement ran though Emily. Just a couple of days ago, she'd have hated to hear Rory –

or anybody – call her a farmer. She'd have been really annoyed. But now, she was so happy she was almost bursting.

'Baa-aaa!' Lizzie was awake. She was trying to stand up on the cushion, while Patch licked her anxiously.

'Time for breakfast,' Rory said. He pulled a bottle of milk out of his pocket and gave it to Emily. 'You know what to do. I'll go back to the farmhouse and rustle up something for us humans.'

He was just going to the door when there was a loud clatter of feet outside in the farmyard. Jack and Asha had arrived.

'We're early, I know!' Asha gasped. 'But we wanted to see Curly! Is she OK?'

'I woke up thinking about her,' Jack added. 'I just had to come in right away.'

'Baa-aaa!' called Lizzie from the cushion.

Asha and Jack jumped in surprise and stared at her with their mouths open.

'It's Curly's baby!' Asha squealed.

'Yes. A little ewe. Curly gave birth just before midnight,' Rory said.

'Why isn't she with her mum?' Jack frowned.

Rory explained that Curly had had a very tough time with the birth. He told Jack and Asha that both she and the lamb might have died.

'But thanks to Emily, who told me what was happening, all is well. The vet came. Curly's had some medicine and she's going to be fine.'

'What about the lamb?' Jack asked.

'Emily's in charge.' Rory winked at her. 'Perhaps she'd like to show Asha how to bottle-feed, while we go and check up on the ewe?'

'I'll come,' Mr Keane said. 'I've got to meet the famous Curly, star of the farmyard.'

'You saw her before, Dad, when we first came,' Emily said.

She didn't want him to go. The thought of being alone with Asha made her feel uncomfortable. What if she was still upset?

'Yes – but we haven't been properly introduced yet!' Mr Keane chuckled, as he followed Rory and Jack out of the barn.

Emily looked at Asha. She was wearing her woolly hat today, with matching mittens, and a long, grey overcoat that hung down to the ground and looked like it might have belonged to her grandad. Her eyes were shining with excitement as she watched Lizzie and Patch. She didn't seem unhappy to be alone with Emily.

Emily gave her the bottle and they went over to the cushion. Lizzie was baa-ing loudly again.

'Wow,' Asha breathed. 'She's the cutest thing I've ever seen!'

'No, not like that,' Emily said, as Asha went to pick Lizzie up and cuddle her. She showed Asha how to grip the baby ewe between her knees and then hold the bottle above her head. 'That's right! Just as if she was feeding from her mum.'

Asha followed Emily's instructions, and the lamb grabbed the teat of the bottle in her mouth and sucked it hard.

'Good girl, Lizzie!' Emily cried.

Asha looked puzzled. 'Lizzie?'

Emily felt shy again. 'I named her after my mum.'

'Cool!' Asha grinned at her. 'Lizzie the lamb! Brilliant. Do you want to take over now? You're the expert.'

'No, it's OK.'

Emily's head was spinning with relief. Asha wasn't upset any more about how rude Emily'd been. She was perfectly friendly again, happy and relaxed.

'Keep going, Asha. The milk's nearly all gone, look!'

'This is the most exciting thing ever!' Asha sighed.

'I wish Jack could see me now.'

In spite of the cold, damp weather, Jack was sweating with nerves as he hurried down the path with Rory and Mr Keane. What if the vet was wrong and the ewe had taken a turn for the worse?

'I wish I'd been here last night,' he said, as they arrived at the stable.

'It would've been great to have you around,' Rory told him. 'You and Emily would've made a great team.'

Jack was about to say that he wasn't sure he'd want to be on any team with Emily, but Rory was already opening the door.

Curly was standing up, munching greedily on some hay.

'Wow!' Jack said.

Rory grinned. 'Yup. Right as rain.'

'Baaa!' Curly said, as if she was agreeing with them. She blinked her golden-brown eyes and trotted over to Jack, nuzzling at his pocket.

'Here you are.' He pulled out a packet of Polos. 'Your favourite treat!'

'It's hard to believe there was anything wrong with her,' Mr Keane said, as Curly took the mint from the palm of Jack's hand and crunched it up. 'What about Lizzie? If her mum's better, shouldn't they be together?'

Jack gave Curly another Polo. 'She might not want her baby now,' he said.

'Why not?' Mr Keane looked surprised.

'Jack's right. Often a ewe will reject a lamb that she's been separated from. She won't recognize the smell of it, if it's been handled by humans.' Rory looked thoughtful. 'But it might be worth a try. And I know just the person who might be able to bring Curly and her baby back together.'

Emily hugged Lizzie to her chest as Rory opened the door to Curly's stable.

'Be careful!' Jack warned her. 'Curly might be upset. She might attack the lamb, if she doesn't recognize her.'

Emily felt confused. Half of her wanted Lizzie to go back to Curly and half of her wanted to keep the tiny creature and go on caring for her.

Rory nodded. 'It's possible. But we've wiped Lizzie down with a clean cloth, so she doesn't smell too much of dogs or humans. There's a chance Curly'll know her again.'

'Baaa!' The ewe looked round from her hay.

Lizzie wriggled in Emily's arms and answered 'Baa-aaa!' in her own little voice.

Curly listened, her golden-brown eyes shining.

Rory watched her. Then he said, 'I think it might be OK. Ready, Emily?'

Emily nodded. Lizzie bleated again. She wanted to get down and run to her mum.

Rory patted Emily's shoulder. 'Let them take their time. Don't interfere. We'll keep out of the way, but we're here if you need us.'

Emily stepped inside the stable and Rory shut the door behind her. She put Lizzie down, and the lamb stood up on her wobbly legs. Curly stared at her.

'Baa-aaa!' Lizzie staggered towards Curly. She wasn't used to walking, and after a few steps she flopped down in the straw.

Emily wanted to help, but she remembered what Rory'd said. *Don't interfere.* She waited.

Lizzie untangled her long legs and managed to stand up again. Curly had a worried expression on her face.

'It's your baby, Curly,' Emily said.

Curly looked at Emily. Then she looked at Lizzie again. 'Baaa!' she said. She walked over to the lamb and sniffed her head.

Emily held her breath.

Curly was licking Lizzie now, all over her little body.

It was going to be all right!

Lizzie staggered and almost fell over again. Emily laughed.

'Careful, Curly!' she said. 'You'll knock her over!'

But Lizzie was getting stronger on her feet. When she'd been licked clean, she walked all round her mum, looking for the udder.

'Left a bit – no, right a bit!' Emily said, trying not to laugh.

At last Lizzie found the milk she was so hungry for, and began to suck.

'Hurray,' Asha whispered, looking over the door. She clapped her mittened hands together in silent applause.

'Wow. Brilliant, Emily,' Jack said.

When Lizzie had finished drinking, the ewe and lamb lay down in the straw together. There was no need for Emily to stay in the stable. She felt a pang of sadness that she'd never feed the tiny lamb from the bottle again. But Lizzie and Curly looked so happy.

Jack and Asha were waiting for her outside.

'Where's Rory and my dad?' Emily asked.

She felt awkward and shy. She'd thought so many mean things about Jack, and been so rude to Asha. How would they behave towards her?

'They're making breakfast,' Asha said, with a little skip. 'Come on, I'm starving. You must be too, Emily.'

Jack's eyes were bright with admiration as they walked up to the farmhouse. 'It was great, the way you left Curly and the lamb alone, and didn't fuss. You were so patient. Rory's dead right. You're really good with animals.'

Emily's face was hot. They were both being so friendly to her. She felt really bad.

'I've been so rude,' she said. 'Especially to you, Asha. I'm really sorry.'

Asha grinned. 'Thanks! But I've forgotten about it now. Anyway, you couldn't help it. You were feeling bad about your mum.'

Jack nodded. 'It must have been awful to lose her,' he said. 'I remember when my grandad got ill and we had to leave Hilltop Farm. I thought I'd never be happy again.' Then he chuckled. 'And I was just as nasty as you. You should've heard me when I first came to City Farm. I thought it was a silly little dump, after being at Hilltop. And I was angry with everybody. I was scared they'd call me stupid.'

Asha grinned. 'Crazy boy! You might not be the best at reading and writing, but you're dead smart.'

'Smart enough not to get angry any more,' Jack replied. 'Or not to take it out on other people, at least.'

'This is the best place ever,' Asha said. 'I feel great now, but after my treatment for leukaemia I was so tired I just lay on the sofa all the time. I didn't even want to watch telly. My mum was really worried about me because I wouldn't eat all the food she kept cooking.'

Emily was surprised to hear this, even though she knew Asha'd been ill. 'But you're always busy now. You never stop running around and talking and—'

'Eating!' Jack interrupted.

It's true!' Asha giggled. 'I'm starving every minute of the day.'

'Remember the time you broke the record for eating the most flapjacks in the café?' Jack teased her.

Asha giggled even more. Her laugh was so infectious that Emily couldn't help joining in. It was really funny to picture Asha stuffing her face with flapjacks. She clutched her sides and gasped for breath. It was so long since she had laughed like this. Patch jumped up and licked her hand, her eyes shining. Emily looked at Jack and Asha's happy faces, grinning at her with delight.

I'm not lonely any more, she thought, as they raced up the path together. *I've got three of the best friends in the world…*

'Hey, kids!' her dad was calling from the front door of the farmhouse. 'Who wants a bacon butty? There's veggie sausages too. And beans, eggs and mushrooms!'

Emily, Jack and Asha ran towards him, with Patch leaping at their heels. As they sat down at the big table in the farmhouse kitchen, Patch crept underneath and sat on Emily's feet.

'She's not trembling,' Emily said. 'I don't think she's quite so scared to be near other people any more.'

Rory was serving out the food, his face redder than ever from cooking. 'It's the City Farm effect. Works every time,' he chuckled.

Emily's dad smiled at her from across the table, as he helped himself to a large bacon roll.

She smiled back. Underneath the table, something soft brushed against her ankle. It was Patch, wagging her tail to show she was happy too.

Epilogue

One morning, two weeks later, Emily was in the hall at her dad's house. She was helping Denise get Leon ready to go out.

'Shall I put his boots on?'

She loved her baby brother's cute yellow wellingtons. They made him look like a miniature fireman.

'Why not?' Denise said, peering into the mirror to check her lipstick. 'It's not raining right now, but he does like wearing them.'

'Mmmm!' Leon chortled, as Emily pushed his feet into the boots and lifted him into his pushchair.

Emily giggled. '*Mmmm?* What's that supposed to mean? Are you trying to say "Mum"?'

Leon roared with laughter.

Denise grinned at the two of them. 'If he's saying

 133

anything, I think it must be "Emily".'

'Are we ready?' Mr Keane came hurrying down the stairs, taking them two at a time. He had the morning off work, because it was Emily's first day back at school.

'Yup!' Denise replied. 'All set.'

'You feeling OK, Emily?' her dad asked.

A few butterflies were flitting around in her stomach, but Emily didn't feel too bad at the thought of going back to her new school. She was sure she would make at least one friend there now. And every weekend she'd be able to go back to City Farm and catch up with Asha and Jack, and the animals. Especially Curly and Lizzie.

'I'm fine, Dad,' she said, and the butterflies stopped flitting quite so much. 'Let's go.'

Her dad and Denise had promised to walk to school with her, so she didn't feel lonely.

'Hang on. We're forgetting someone…' Mr Keane reached up to the coat rack on the wall and took down a blue dog lead.

'Oh, no! How could I? Where's she hiding?' Emily grabbed the lead. 'Patch! Walkies!'

With a skitter of claws across the floor, the black and white dog came racing through from the kitchen, where she'd been lying in her bed next to the tumble dryer. She leaped up to lick Emily's chin.

Emily told her to sit, and then she clipped on her lead. 'You've got to come too,' she said.

'Mmmm-mm!' said Leon, beaming and reaching his arms out to them.

Emily laughed. 'Now he's saying "Patch"!'

'She's part of the family now, our Patch,' Mr Keane smiled.

The sun was shining as the five of them set off along the road towards the school. There was blossom on the branches of the trees, and Leon shouted and waved from his pushchair at the colourful daffodils and tulips that were flowering in the front gardens of the houses. Patch wagged her tail and stayed close to Emily's heels.

Emily said goodbye at the school gates. She watched them walking back along the pavement. Her dad and Denise were holding hands, and Patch was trotting proudly next to the pushchair. *My family are great*, she thought. *They're really cool.*

She turned to go into the school building. A group of girls ran past her, laughing. Emily picked up her bag and ran with them, ready to start her first day back.

CHARACTER PROFILE

ANIMAL: **Puppy**
ANIMAL NAME: **Patch**

LIKES:

Playing with Emily, long walks, playing fetch.

DISLIKES:

Loud noises, being cold.

FAVOURITE PLACE:

The end of Emily's bed.

FAVOURITE FOOD:

Gravy bones and other doggy treats.

Turn over for a sneak peek of the next
City Farm adventure...

Zoe and Swift

Zoe stared at the white ceiling. She had pulled the curtains round her bed, shutting out the busy ward with the nurses bustling about, the parents talking, the little kids playing. With the curtains closed, she felt like she was in her own little world. She wished she could stay there. She didn't feel like ever going outside again.

Catching sight of the plaster cast that covered her right leg from her knee to her toes, she shut her eyes. Her mind filled with pictures of the last race she'd run. She remembered the feeling of speed, passing the other runners, crossing the finishing line. Afterwards her coach had come up to her and told her that if she kept running like that she'd be in the Olympics one day. It had been one of the happiest days of Zoe's life.

She'd been daydreaming about the Olympics in the car on the way home – and then someone had driven into Mum's car.

The doctors had explained that her leg had been so badly broken that she would have to wear a cast for several months. She would then have to have physiotherapy and would probably walk with a limp for the rest of her life. It would be a long time before she raced again, if ever.

Lying there, Zoe felt empty. Like everything inside her had been ripped away, leaving an empty, hollow space. Tears started to creep down her cheeks. She scrubbed them angrily away.

'Hi, sweetheart.'

The curtains pushed aside and Mum looked in. She looked like an older version of Zoe, tall and skinny with dark skin and long braided hair. She was smiling, but Zoe could see the strain in the lines around her eyes.

'Hi, Mum,' Zoe managed, having to force the words past the lump in her throat.

'Well, today's the big day. It's time to come home.' Mum smiled brightly.

Zoe bit her lip as she thought about going back to her house. She was looking forward to going home, but she felt funny about it too. It would be like nothing had changed, when everything had.

Her mum must have seen the misery on her face. 'Oh, Zoe,' she said softly, crossing to the top of the bed and fiddling with Zoe's braids. 'I know it's really hard for you but you'll feel better when you get back home. I promise you will. We've made the study downstairs into your bedroom now so you won't have to go up the stairs and you'll soon feel like your usual, cheerful self. Things will start getting back to normal.'

'Normal?' Zoe said bleakly.

'Yes, normal.'

Zoe turned her head away. Her mum was trying to be nice, she knew that, but she had no idea. Absolutely no idea at all. Normal? No. One thing was for sure. Her life was never going to be normal again…

Read

Zoe and Swift

to find out what happens next!

Our *City Farm* and the *Harvest Hope* project
are fictional, but there are real city farms
all around the country and they often
need volunteers. Why not go and visit the
one nearest to you?

For more exciting books from brilliant
authors, follow the fox!
www.curious-fox.com